If Walls could Weep

If Walls could Weep

NANDITA BOSE

LiFi PUBLICATIONS PVT. LTD.
NEW DELHI

Published by:
LiFi Publications Pvt. Ltd.
211, 2nd Floor, Gagandeep
12, Rajendra Place, New Delhi–110 008, India
Phone : (011) 2574 1000
E-mail : info@lifipublications.com
Web : www.lifipublications.com

ISBN 13: 978-93-82536-43-7 ISBN 10: 93-82536-43-4

First published in 2014

Cataloging in Publication Data—DK
[Courtesy: D.K. Agencies (P) Ltd. <docinfo@dkagencies.com>]

Bose, Nandita, 1964–
If walls could weep / Nandita Bose.
p. cm.
Novel.
ISBN 9789382536437

1. Kolkata (India)--Fiction. 2. Indic fiction (English). I. Title.

DDC 823.92 23

Printed in India by D.K. Fine Art Press (P) Ltd., Delhi–52

Acknowledgement

Writers perish in isolation. Our community keeps us alive. The first and most important community is our community of readers. I cannot adequately express the immense high of readers writing in and telling me how deeply my story touched them. That fuels our meanderings, proves a powerful motivation for us to keep chipping away at this most difficult and perhaps most irrelevant of life paths.

And then there are other writers whose experiences and talents sometimes mirror and sometimes enhance our own. My first taste of this had been at the Bangalore Literary Festival 2013 where I was especially blown away by the grace, generosity and acceptance from stalwarts like Bhawana Somaaya, Gita Aravumudan, Farah Ghuznavi, Farooq Shaheen, Munni Nasreen, Nighat Gandhi, Nilanjan Choudhury, Vasanthi Hariprakash, Ravi Subramanian, Piyush Jha, Satyajit Sarna and Sobha Narayan.

For this high point of my brief career as a writer I must thank the organisers of the BLF: Shinie Antony, Vikram

Sampath and Srikrishna Ramamoorthy, their amazing team of dedicated volunteers and all who prioritised the written word above all else those three days of the festival.

Special mention is deserved by my mentor/ angels within Bangalore who have created these little oases of creativity and intellectual interaction: Vani Mahesh of EasyLib and Lakshmi and Subodh Shankar of Atta Galatta.

My thoughts also run to Chethana Dinesh of Deccan Herald whose encouragement gives impetus in a new direction that I find myself enjoying, that of a literary reviewer.

The people who are extended family for me and my kids, who I can call any time of the night or day and choose to spend my leisure hours with, are perhaps my greatest indicator of wealth: Rachna and Alok Singh, Shubha Ramachandran and Sameer Shisodia, Bindu Mandira and Sumit Sharma, Sujata Shrivastava and Anupam Bharteeya, Priya and Rohit Sharma.

I have come a long way with the sustained blessings and help from loving elders such as Promita and Subrato Banerjee, Abanti and Barin Sanyal.

And from back in Jamshedpur and my early days in Mumbai there are so many friends who have been there for me down the years: Shreevalli Countcham, Rita Chakraborty, Soum Chakraborty, Avijit Nandi, Anuj Gandhi, Asha Nandkumar, Urvashi Kamalia, Anuradha Khan, Archana Dekate, Karuna Chavan, Ipsita Chatterjee, Vinod Philip, Harmit Singh Malik, Mangesh Mahajan, Vivek Pathak, Ghane, Mansab, Yut and perhaps far too many to name individually.

I must mention my first and most enthusiastic reader, my cousin Subhra Paul Chaudhuri who I can always count on and my wonderful nephew, Joydip Ghosh Roy, who has been such a wonderful and much needed support.

From my extended universe on Facebook are friends who were total strangers till a while back and have today become fellow travellers on my journeys.

A lot of the universe's mysteries are revealed by my Gurus: Professor Milind Malshe, Parag Vyas, Sritha Mahagatha and Sromona Charkaborty.

At the risk of sounding repetitive I must reiterate my deep indebtedness to the author Shinie Antony for being a quiet, positive and powerful guardian angel, not only for me but for a huge network of writers in Bangalore and beyond.

And once again to Rachna Singh, for always being there.

For a book to achieve a physical entity, it requires the trust and commitment of publishers. It is a matter of pride to see up close the great professionalism and vision of the entire team at LiFi Publications.

I live in the most wonderful household surrounded by love and care, laughter and happiness. For this invaluable resource and for putting up with my erratic schedules and needs I must thank my daughters, Rashi and Reeti Kumar. And for the man who gave me wings, Kumar Ramachandran.

Prologue

At one of the bleakest moments of my life I sat outdoors late into the night looking up at the freezing stars and asking myself questions too complicated for my young mind to tackle. The questions all had to do with the deep unhappiness in me, with my sense of loss and longing, with concerns for my well being and future.

I hadn't planned on these questions recurring. Yet they did, with alarming regularity.

Why is love elusive? And why is it synonymous with a thousand betrayals? Why is it that everyone seeks it and yet no one actually knows its worth? Why is there never enough love? Why is love never enough?

In this crowded chaotic ruthless pathway of pain that we call life, so many things offer themselves as substitutes for love. We seek it in objects or goals easier to have and hold. We seek it in temporary highs. We seek it in what makes us feel numb or distracted until it is time to confront our lonely and empty selves again.

In time some answers appeared. Not solutions. Just a kind of blurred understanding of things. Like how life is always a seeking. The seeking remains, lifelong. It is in modifying that search that we find our moments of bliss and our sources of strength. These modifications come to us through struggle as learning. And the most profound learning is this: it is all about love.

Yes, it does seem like a cyclical paradox. In living a life of love and compassion we find our own salvation. And sometimes, almost too rare to be true, our prayers are answered. We don't find that perfect someone. We find someone special who is reasonably committed to our presence, our happiness and to our love. And together we navigate the joys and the surprises of that playground called life.

what epics hide weighed under
brick and mortar or in the living
souls deep

the slow tragedies of lives betrayed
grow hesitant soft moss
with rains that seep

what dirges pure and primal
would float on evening air
if walls could weep

1

Bula: 46 years

There is something heady about celebration outdoors. It harks back to countless dim nights in prehistory: fires, roasting of some unspecified carcass, intoxicants either brewed or botanical, heaving emotions, people all around, sparks and either subdued or rhythmic frenzy. This celebration in the now may appear a far cry. But appearances are not always what they seem.

Garden of Eden is an upscale restaurant in the heart of Kolkata ensconced among fairly elegant neighbours of boutiques, exclusive showrooms, an art gallery and a multiplex among others. On the afternoon of *Mahashtami*, the sacred eighth day of the *Navratri Durga* puja, among numerous other patrons at lunch, sits a family that somehow warrants a second glance. Perhaps it is the special care three dedicated waiters are lavishing on just placing the chilled water goblets for the five occupants of the table or the frequent visits by the manager, Shantanu Chaudhuri, to check everything is alright.

Your eye is drawn to the magnetic personality of this distinguished-looking gentleman. You may not place him immediately but in certain quarters Nikhil Mitra is a powerful figure.

Beside him sits a delicate-featured, attractive man of about twenty. The way he holds himself, the slant of his shoulders and his quiet assurance would hint to you that he is a model or an actor. And you'd be right; Tathagata Mitra is an upcoming stage actor in this city where that glowing heritage has slowly all but decayed.

'After all this, Bula, he wants to be an actor!'

'Nikhil, if we can't support our son in any career he chooses, who can?'

'I don't feel comfortable about this. I just don't.'

'My next project will be to build him a theatre and help him set up his own repertory. Don't worry, it will turn out alright.'

Newer project plans were no longer the stuff of nightmares, but that didn't leave Nikhil completely unalarmed either. Now he'd chosen the prudent path of silence.

Milky white glasses of the house speciality are now being served at the table. It is tender coconut water blended with the delicate, still jellylike coconut bloom. She takes a tentative sip, likes it and drinks deeper. To Nikhil's left she sits, her complexion and features so seem to match his that she can only be his daughter. What biology denies sometimes real life makes true as that resemblance is nothing but the oddest of coincidences. You'd notice that in that roomful of the best-dressed elite, she wears simple handspun clothes, *Kolhapuri chappals*, glass beaded earrings and a couple of glass bangles on her wrist. Carelessly flopped beside her chair is that hallmark of the Bengali intellectual, the cloth *jhola*. Geetanjali Banerjee, the girls use their mother's maiden surname, appears regularly in the papers too. Though you would not expect that Geetanjali to be dining at an overtly opulent place as this. And you would notice her being ill at ease. Only her love for the family having brought her here.

For Geetanjali is the firebrand founder and chief activist of the Green Bengal Movement, a popular environmental organisation for the youth where college students and young professionals volunteer to provide environment-friendly solutions across West Bengal. In reality she often pickets la di da commercial spaces such as these for their rampant disregard of environment norms. Not that Garden of Eden could even be remotely considered in that bracket. She had long dinned into her Uncle Akhil all the compliance norms until he could recite them fluently.

To her left beyond an empty chair, sits the oldest child, Debjani. Though clad in a grey and gold silk saree with passable grace, it somehow does not mask the fact that she is at her best in business suits. After having completed her studies in engineering and at the topmost management institute in the state, she has chosen to join her parents' business at the entry level, currently managing the oldest Sealdah rice godown. She is an indefatigable worker leaving her parents elated that with her the business has a future into the next generation. The only sore point is the topic of finding her a life partner.

'There just aren't men like Nikhil anymore, Ma.'

'I'm sure there are other kinds of suitable men, Debjani. How long can you live alone? As it is, I am so worried about Akhil.'

'And why am I being discussed here?' a smiling Akhil asked as he sat down between Debjani and his *Bou-di* after smothering the former in a bear hug as greeting. Another gentleman in an eye-popping vermillion kurta occupied the seat between the two girls. He was Niranjan Datta.

'Sorry *Dada,* Bou-di, we got a little late inside. Just some last minute instructions in the kitchen and all.'

Akhil looked around and caught Shantanu's eye. Being kept waiting at the table made him mournful and it was a smallish almost doleful note as he spoke.

'Shantanu, feed us please.'

The impeccable surroundings saw to it that the revels could not really be raucous. But it came as close to that as possible. This table was intent on having fun, a happy family celebrating this occasion and their lives together. Even the normally reticent waiters loosened, smiling and bantering.

After the leisurely lunch the two younger men and the kids needed to leave. Only Tathagata dawdled, leaning forward and speaking low to his mother.

'See you in the evening, Ma.'

She held him to her with her eyes closed to feel him better. All moms are said to be partial to their youngest and their sons and that seemed to be borne out amply here.

'Make sure Akhil drives carefully. And take care in the crowds.'

He nodded and then stood up stiffly to be excused by his Dad.

'Niru, take plenty of pictures for us. We can't go into the immense crowds of the *pandals* anymore.'

'Yes, and Bou-di, we should be home around eight or so for dinner with you.'

'Happy pandal-hopping, all of you!'

'And Akhil, drive that damn SUV carefully.'

As he left laughing, Akhil said over his shoulder:

'Dada, just remember with all my reckless driving I've never had an accident, unlike some others I could name.'

Nikhil sat down on the chair left vacant by Tathagata. The table was swiftly cleared. The manager hovered nearby.

'Shantanu, could I have some tea?'

Tea was brought in a pot. The staff here knew as did everyone, that Nikhil only drank tea prepared by Bou-di. She poured and handed him his cup a little slow, almost weighed down by her thoughts.

'What are you thinking about, Bula?'

'Nothing. Am just enjoying the peace, now that the mob has left.'

Something flashed as the cup changed hands. A blaze of iced fire from the oval diamond ring she wore.

You would then look at this woman called Bula Banerjee, rumoured to be as acute a businessperson as Nikhil Mitra. Too little is really known about her except that she is an equal partner in that huge conglomerate. You would observe her carefully. Her greying hair is cut elegantly up to the shoulders. At her ears, sparkle solitaires. That mild sheen of the red-bordered cream silk softly speaks of luxury belied by its simplicity. In every way she seems to have led a sheltered, protected life, pampered by a lifetime of wealth and luck. How enviably simple some people's lives are!

When it is time to leave, Nikhil asks for the bill. Shantanu looks distinctly unhappy.

'Akhil-da or Niru-da or even their friends never pay, even though they eat here every day.'

'They work here, Shantanu. It is theirs.'

'How can I charge you Nikhil-da? On an occasion like this.'

That settled, they left the terrace restaurant and stepped into the waiting silver Mercedes. Dhanraj turned around and asked them where they wanted to go.

'Home!' they replied in unison and turned and smiled at each other.

'Sorry Dhanraj, you had to work today. Once you drop us back, you can take the rest of the day off.'

'It's okay. Leave is not necessary for me, Dada Babu.'

Settling in the car, the poised Nikhil unbent, sat sloppy in the softness of his seat prompting Bula to edge in closer. The softly scented interiors and the ease of that noiseless ride rested them for a while.

'Nikhil?'

'Hmmm?'

'For some time now, I've wanted to write an autobiography of our lives.'

'Heaven forbid!'

'Not that tired old business tycoon's special secrets to get rich, quick kind of ghost-written book.'

'What do you have in mind?'

'A kind of novel, simply written, about our story: yours and mine.'

'Do you even have the time, Bula, now that your love for your son has made you over-commit to the theatre project? And what is the use anyway? Strangers will then know about our lives.'

'If I can manage to write it well, it will be a testimony to our lives and perhaps what makes it all worthwhile.'

'Isn't it enough for you to just feel it and have it reciprocated?' I just shook my head, slowly.

✦ ✦ ✦

2

Bula: 21 years

Krishnapur is like a tiny town nestling alongside numerous other towns loosely connected into a conglomerate called Kolkata. There are really no special features that make it unique. Just a couple of mandatory tanks, a few temples, small markets interspersed, a bus stand and the token grammar and high schools – separate timings for boys and girls. It is at a sufficient distance from the city centre to have an autonomous life. Change percolates here with utmost difficulty.

When the financial troubles went beyond her endurance, my distraught *Ma* had me sent away to her brother's place here. By then I had my own reasons for wishing for an exile. The humble rooms I came to stay at were thus a merciful luxury. My uncle rented one bit portion of the third floor in a rambling damp building that was slowly going to seed. My aunt shared distinctly uncordial relations with all her fellow tenants. Though I think her daily dramatic encounters with them all provided her with much of the excitement her mundane existence craved.

My Uncle and Aunt were nice. I was truly grateful to them for having taken me in when I most needed somewhere else to be. Yet the dissociation from my life as it had been so far was too great. I was mostly struggling to just remain calm outwardly. And be the least bother possible.

Within my first week there I discovered the kaleidoscopic beauty of the terrace view. Myriad rooftops stretched into the horizon, suspended concrete tiers in skyspace. Whenever I got the chance I would escape there and revel in the boundless freedom this place seemed to offer. That respite was needed as the metropolis was otherwise suffocating.

Beyond way past the pond area and the main road, was a small tract of unoccupied land bustling with coconut palms. Through the gaps in the fronds further stood a large handsome mansion. Its paint seemed more recent than any building nearby though it too had patches of fine green-black moss that was common to this locality. That building stood rooted in a deep sense of grace only a good architect could impart. What really made it special were the huge grounds. From my uncertain vantage on our terrace I saw a patchwork of beautiful gardens with tall trees and flowering bushes.

My curiosity about that particular place simmered intermittently until late one morning, when I came to the terrace with the large pail of clothes I'd been washing, my aunt followed. Her hair, for the moment tied turban-like in the red checked cloth towel, was to be dried out with care. As I strung the clothes on the line, her quick eyes caught me glancing at the mansion.

'Isn't that house lovely? It is Tarapada Babu's mansion. Very rich people.'

'I see.'

'Tarapada Babu is quiet and gruff, but good at heart, a philanthropist. He has been providing food and shelter for his partner's family for years and years now. Lost his wife, the poor man. Now the house is run by that other lady. My, is she a shrew! Very terrible. And so uppity too. Won't even look at people like us.'

I made more non-committal noises.

'Between the two families there are five boys, all good boys except for Tara Babu's oldest son. Nikhil, I think he is called. Was known to be somewhat of a brains but grew up to be very quiet and snobbish. Keeps to himself all the time. Won't greet his elders or anything.'

'Shall I dry your hair?'

My aunt happily settled on this cot that had been left to the elements on the terrace to bleach and warp. I vigorously rubbed her hair with the hopelessly inadequate sodden rag of a towel.

✦

Food was the only focus of life in my Uncle's house. He would wake up early to go and get the best pickings as cheap as possible in the market nearby. Amid the bustling and haggling there, discussing the merits and demerits of the wares of fish and vegetables had been elevated to an art form. After coming home with bags laden with fresh produce he would fuss over everyone in the house, including me. Then he would complete a ritual of shaving with a small plastic bowl of warm water, his trusty shaving kit and Dettol as aftershave. Once done, he would sit on a tin folding chair in the passage outside the kitchen and read the newspaper. For every news item he read he would shout out a concise commentary for his wife bustling about in the tiny kitchen by then.

My aunt was a good cook and produced incredible delicacies on a daily basis from her vast repertoire. It was quite usual for all of us to stuff ourselves at lunch. My aunt would invariably be the worst offender needing to retire for a heavy nap. In the afternoons the muggy Kolkata air thickened and stilled all movement. Uneasy as I was with the gastronomic delights inside of me, I would succumb and lie down for a bit too.

I was lost in just such a brown haze of blankness when all the wooden shutters in the building began to bang furiously in an unexpected gale. The outsides were a threatening grey with black rain clouds ready to open up any moment. There were tons of washing drying on the terrace. I needed to run up, wrestle with the swollen recalcitrant door and rescue what I could out in the terrace. The clothes whipped around in the wind like the possessed. And I had a merry dance trying to hold and gather them all.

Out of habit I turned towards the mansion. On its terrace stood a young man, lean, somehow very alone, his hands soberly crossed over his middle. The wind whipped wildly at his white kurta. In that vast expanse all around us, no one else was around, just the furious rising gale. It was a raging almost unreal display of the elements' violence. And yet he stood still, imperturbable. I felt certain he had noticed me, as I had. Somehow that thought seemed comforting, like a secret.

It had all happened with bizarre haste. A neighbour, Shefali, asked me to come along to the local shops to help select a saree. My aunt acquiesced. We were just about to enter a narrow lane in the market place which was chock-a-block with tiny stalls.

'How are you, Shefali?' a male voice asked.

We turned around to find this mildly balding, weak-chinned man smiling up at her toothily.

'Aukhoy Babu! I am very well. Hope everything is well with all of you.'

'Won't you introduce me to your friend?'

'Oh she...she is a visitor, from Phuleshwar. Her name is Sulochona.'

I was subjected to an unblinking stare for perhaps too long. It made me mildly uncomfortable but then I forgot that little incident.

Life went on as usual. A scarce postcard from Ma scrawled on each last bit of space kept us connected. I tried not to feel heartsick. The smile got harder to hold on to. Mostly, I tried not to be a nuisance to my uncle and aunt. I worked hard at helping my aunt with all her chores until except for the actual cooking she abdicated the rest of it all to me. I was okay. Hard work is a way of life when money is scarce. One evening however, a messenger called Chaudhuri Babu came to meet us. Bankim Babu from the mansion wanted to meet my uncle. Completely bewildered, my uncle agreed and a suitable time was fixed. During the meeting he was asked by Bankim Babu:

'Will you donate your niece to our household so that like Lakshmi she will bring us prosperity and happiness?'

Unable to comprehend what was happening but thunderstruck at the momentous offer, he had readily accepted.

A careworn Ma and a distant Baba came down to hurriedly conduct the nuptial rites. A hundred and fifty guests came from the groom's side while from mine there were only thirty, including the neighbours my aunt detested.

In the days leading up to the wedding, lots had been done and said. To all around me I was the luckiest person they had seen. I was a fairy story come true, a Cinderella who had found her Prince Charming. People were born, married and died within the sliver-thin confines of their own class, extremely fortunate if they did not fall into the waiting maws of poverty as my mother had done.

Shefali had been furious. She called me all kinds of names accusing me of having manipulated her into introducing myself into the life of this unattainable man of her dreams. One cranky old unmarried aunt of my mother's asked everyone all around what the man could possibly have seen in me!

The wedding itself was somewhat strange. It was held in a hired community hall that seemed cynical about all that it had witnessed in the name of marriage. That contempt expressed by this thick fog of unpleasant smells and a dark brooding light. It seemed to me the various ceremonies were heavily curtailed or rushed through until at midnight itself, I was expected to leave with that family. This went against the grain of established rites but no one thought of protesting. They were a rich and powerful family and whatever they chose to do was just right.

And the same house that I had admired not long back, now grim and forbidding at midnight, turned out much too huge on closer acquaintance. For a building that grand, the inner portions seemed somehow sad and neglected. In fact it was positively desolate when I was directed to go in from a large outer hall and had stepped into what seemed like unending deserted space. I stood there trying to fathom what next when someone appeared in the lit doorway on the opposite arm.

'Upstairs,' she pointed to a stairwell to my left. And further volunteered. 'Second floor.'

Then she was gone. Though nothing in her voice or manner suggested it, I guess she was being kind. There was some oblique light up to the first floor but the ascent to the second was accomplished in pitch dark. My feet faltered, apprehensive. Once at the landing, a dim light on the far passageway outlined the walls and the pillars. Only one doorway seemed ajar and half-welcoming. I stood uncertain whether I was to go towards it when a powerful light was switched on and voices and footsteps came up behind me. A petulant male voice cried out:

'But I don't want to share my room with a woman.'

'Not here, Kishore! Not now.'

This caution came low, in a cold authoritative female voice. I was swept with the duo towards the waiting room. Hostile gazes pierced me. Then the lady spoke.

'You heard, didn't you? My son was forced into this. All of it was under duress. His adamant father threatened to send him away to join the army otherwise. Seems, Kishore had seen you somewhere. What else would he find in a marketplace?'

Here she sniffed her disapproval. I think back to that moment sometimes. I had stood quiet; with no sense of shock or incredulity, just a quiet acceptance. It represents perhaps the first intimation of my adulthood. Belligerent mothers-in-law were the norm rather than the exception. Just that you didn't quite expect a full blast of that hostility in the very first encounter. Visions of comfort and, if not happiness, just a vague sense of settledness drifted away much like a helium balloon from a child's grasp.

I didn't focus on any of that. Given my capricious irreverent mind, I just battled extremely incongruous images of that weedy chinless man in army fatigues. My mother-in-law found a rolled straw mat behind a door and thrust it out at me. I was to sleep at the edge of the room.

'Outside there is a bathroom. Now go remove all that ridiculous make-up!'

There was anger, contempt and everything unpleasant in her voice. When I returned she was sitting on the bed next to her prone son, commiserating and offering advice in equal measure. I don't know when she left the room. Didn't care to. I'd floated off into deep sleep as soon as I lay down. Perhaps I needed that escape from reality.

✦ ✦ ✦

3

Bula: 9 years

I cannot believe I was once relieved to marry Aukhoy Babu.

It may have never been, if only Ashu had not done what he had.

I grew up in Phuleshwar. It's a beautiful sleepy town beside a wide, somnolent Ganga. When I was small everyone I knew was into the jute trade. There were about a dozen jute mills in our town. Each household was involved in its trade: cultivating, selling, weaving or serving at the jute mills. My father kept accounts at the largest jute mill in town. We lived in a nice house amid small open ponds in which the thin reed-like jute was grown to supplement income, just as it was for most homes around us.

After the jute had been harvested the ponds did not remain barren. In the rains they filled up with water chestnuts. Sometimes we had deep pink water lilies with fat frogs croaking on their lily pads, upsetting large bobbles of water. When water hyacinth filled the pond they would call in some labourers who would clear the ponds for a fee. Those were unwanted, weeds. Though their flowers were awfully pretty too.

Then one year a strange and beautiful plant began to grow in the smallest of our ponds which I had by then begun to identify as mine. After a while a large tear drop shaped bud appeared.

The next morning as I woke up I rushed to the grounds to see the bud. It had opened out into the most exquisite flower I had ever seen. An enormous blue lotus!

I knew I should be going in for breakfast of puffed rice in sugary milk with a banana mashed in. But I could only stand and stare. Then I wandered all over the grounds till I was at the gate. A small boy stood just outside.

'I have a blue lotus. Do you want to see it?'

'Where?'

'Come, I'll show you.'

'I am not to go near the ponds. My mother says I might fall in.'

'You are afraid of ponds? It's so silly. You should just be a little careful.'

'Do you know how to swim?'

'Of course, don't you? Baba says when I am older I will be strong enough to go for baths with him in the Ganga and swim around too.'

The little boy had stared at the blue lotus for a long time.

'It's very beautiful.'

'I know. I've never seen a blue lotus before. Have you?'

'No. Is this your house?'

'Yes. Where is yours?'

'I live across the road.'

'There are no houses across the road. Oh, you mean the house among the mango orchards. Nobody has lived there all these years.'

'Yes, we lived in Kolkata. Now we have come to live here.'

'Baba went to Kolkata once. He told me it is a big beautiful city. Did you like living there?'

The little boy did not answer.

'My father gave me these marbles.'

He brought out six glass marbles.

'Wow. I like this one the most.'

While the others were colourless orbs with a streak of yellow or blue inside, one was a deep blue sphere that glittered in the sunlight as it lay on his palm.

'What is your name?'

'Ashu. Yours?'

'Bula. I mean my name in school is Sulochona Debi. But you can call me Bula.'

'Bula!' Just then my mother appeared on our small verandah and called me in for breakfast.

✦ ✦ ✦

4

Bula: 21 years

Nothing much altered for me between my stint at my Uncle's and my marital home. In fact among the many people here and the sheer spaciousness of the place, I was smaller than ever, and lonelier. As that last shred of hope you've been clutching at floats away, it deadens you like nothing else can.

Dinner was a stiff elaborate affair at the household. There was a large rectangular dining room on the first floor. All the male members sat down together formally to eat. Typically, my mother-in-law presided over both meals, but dinner was the higher notch in ceremony. I was usually put to work in the kitchen before dinner. Apart from Shraboni and Sujoya, there was no one to help out in the evenings and after the rigours of my day, the lighter kitchen work provided relief. A while later, my instructions were to help carry the food up. And I remained in the shadows of the room, until it was time to carry all of it down again. My father-in-law slowly took to asking me to refill his glass or for another helping of the *dal*. The first time I think my mother-in-law frowned forbiddingly.

In time however, it was accepted that I'd serve in the role of a junior help.

Most evening there were far too many men at dinner. There was little conversation and the meals were lavish but seldom celebrated or even much appreciated. The air was of stoically ploughing through another of life's duties. Typically after dinner the menfolk would go into the gardens, the verandah or to one of the drawing rooms as the weather permitted.

One evening perhaps a month after the wedding I was asked to report there. These were uncommon summons and I had hesitated in the doorway. My father-in-law spoke up:

'Come, *Bou-ma,* you must meet your family properly. All those relatives who have come and gone are not family. These people you see here are.

'This is Tarapada Babu. He is my closest friend: more than a brother and my business partner. This house we call our own is actually his. Twenty years ago when we needed a place to stay, he and Bou-di kindly brought us here. Then Kishore was ten or eleven. And we have been here since, bound together by ever-strengthening ties.

'Touch his feet. He is the oldest, the most respected member of our family.'

Tarapada Babu was extremely tall and thin with close cropped grey hair and distant eyes. He touched me on my head with both palms, in blessing. Sitting close beside him with the air of someone instructed to be present and most reluctantly complying was a young man.

'This is Nikhil, Tarapada Babu's older son, only twenty four years old now. In reality it is he who is running our business these days. Wonderful boy. If you ever need help, any help at all, always approach him.'

Nikhil resembled his father. Features as sharp. Right now he sported a remote expression and wouldn't look at me. From my days there I knew this gentleman normally spoke little, kept busy and stayed away from most interactions in the house. Odd that he was the closest to my age in the household.

'This is Akhil, Tara Babu's other son, now studying in the eleventh, right? Those two misbehaved boys are mine, Amit and Ajit. They are twins. From now on they are all your family.'

Though all the faces and names were familiar, it was a pity none felt like family. My interactions were limited mainly to Kishore Babu and his mother. Either treated me like a slave they had spent far too much on, who had turned out nightmarishly unequal to their expectations.

✦

Aukhoy Babu occupied a set of three rooms on the second floor of the mansion. The outer room was the largest of the three with a small seating area, large forbidding furniture and a huge four-poster bed which he used while I occupied a mat on the floor at nights. The middle room was mostly bare with a collection of storage cupboards. The inner room was actually the smaller half of the room it originally constituted with the middle one and had a comfortable bed. To me that seemed the nicest somehow. It was tucked at the end of this corridor.

After finding the floor cold, hard and uncomfortable especially during the monsoons, I began to occupy the innermost room when no one was around. With his erratic schedule and totally unpredictable ways I thought Aukhoy

Babu did not notice. That emboldened me to kind of move in there. Until very late one night he decided he needed me, and he came pounding on my door and when I opened the door still in the mists of sleep in my eyes after a day of drudgery, he continued his pounding on me and that seemed to give him a better impetus for what he had intended for me.

And that became the tenor of my life. For about six to eight weeks, I was left completely alone by Aukhoy Babu and one night he would come to me and leave me battered, bruised and broken by the morning. Anyone who glanced at me would notice the bruised and bitten marks on my face, hands and especially on the areas around my throat and chest and I tried to pull my saree closer to mask my situation the best I could.

At all other times, Aukhoy Babu passed off as the soul of piety, spending hours in the puja room of the mansion and then all his spare hours in one or the other of the three temples that stood in the locality. At those dinner times when I was asked to be at hand to help my mother-in-law with serving food for the menfolk, he would proudly talk of his exploits at the temples, of how he could soon be a temple managing committee member or how he had been asked to go along to the temple festival at some neighbouring town as his piety had now become a known fact among the right circles.

Only his mother seemed delighted at how important or spiritual and great her son was. She would beam and then egg him on to relate some incident of his triumph. Everyone else tended to just ignore him and his boasts. I noticed there was something almost barmy about his simplistic view of how popular and holy he was. And it was within the passage of a painfully short time that I realised with a sense of despair,

I had the ill fortune of being married to an absolutely weak repugnant man who lacked all redeeming qualities that sustain whatever warmth is required for a relationship.

His mother ran the household. By nature she was mean and authoritarian. Even the servants quaked in her presence. And she tended to treat me with a contempt reserved for someone lesser that a menial there. Her tone and language in addressing me bordered on crude and she ensured that from about dawn to ten in the night I slaved all over the household harder than any maid there.

When Durga puja approached, a mere couple of months after my marriage, this same housemaid Sujoya, little more than a slip of a girl then, summoned me to this informal drawing room. The room was larger then, more imposing.

My father-in-law sat on this chair among a flock of relatives who descended on the household at this time of the year. I stood at the threshold wondering at the summons.

'Come Bou-ma,', he said. 'Tomorrow when you and Kishore go to visit your family, I thought you would like to wear this.'

The box was velvet covered and as I opened it, I was dazed by the glitter of the nine gemstones framed by the dull gold necklace. That perhaps was my only moment of recompense for all broken promises. However, the moment I returned from my Uncle's place, my mother-in-law swooped upon that piece of jewellery too and took it away for "safekeeping".

The retching began maybe a couple of weeks later. I felt weak and dizzy. I could not get out of bed at dawn as I had done all my life. It went on partially unnoticed for a couple more weeks.

One afternoon, the plain fish curry and rice I'd eaten refused to stay down and I ran out beyond the kitchen gardens into the little copse of bushes. As I retched I noticed two washing women who were at the water tank with mounds of the household clothes stare at me open-mouthed.

'Bou-ma is going to have a son soon', they shouted out to me with great amusement.

I was thunderstruck. Was I going to have a baby? In this situation? How could it be?

Don't ask me how I got pregnant...it's not the fondest of my memories. It involved a bitter money-related brawl between him and his mother; another misunderstanding with his friends who came each evening and sat on the verandah eating fried snacks with endless cups of tea; some brute force applied to an unwilling but unresisting partner and a night of dark pain.

Sometimes I felt like informing him about the baby, hoping that news would bring about a small modification of this untenable master-slave equation between us. Even trying to put the thought into words scared me about my future.

Over time I began to feel intense anger. It was an unproductive emotion but it helped fuel me as I was heaped with larger and larger amounts of menial work in the household.

✦ ✦ ✦

5

Bula: 22 years

The puja room was being prepared for a solemn prayer meeting. My mother-in-law had given extensive instructions and had gone off to her afternoon's rest.

I was floundering in the middle of too much to do and a gaggle of maids all needing close monitoring. A large framed picture of a deity that hung above the doorway wore a garland of long-dried flowers. That needed to be replaced. It was too high for me to reach. I stood on tiptoe on a tin folding chair with a walking stick in hand hoping to reach and remove the garland with its curved handle.

'You will fall!' a voice said behind me.

I stopped what I was doing, unsure what to do next.

'Allow me.'

He held out a hand with the air of prime reluctance as he helped me off the chair. He looked at Sujoya to ask:

'Where are Mukunda and Durlabh? Why is the bride doing all this work? Go call them immediately.'

He himself stepped on the rickety chair and with great ease removed the dried flowers. It was much easier to work with Nikhil around. All the servants turned more deferential and efficient. He gave precise orders and knew what needed to be done. I found myself working a lot happier in the midst of this efficient buzz. Then he approached me, carrying a large portrait of his mother. It was for her death anniversary that this prayer meeting was being held.

'I've cleaned it out. Can you apply the sandalwood paste? I'm no good at it.'

The portrait was placed gently on a large carpet as I began preparing the pastes. He sat beside me waiting. Was I supposed to make small talk? Or was it improper to converse? Perhaps I needed to dispel the awkwardness.

'How old were you when your mother passed away?'

'Seven.'

'That little? Do you miss her?'

'Not anymore.'

'Isn't it very lonely, not having a mother?'

'You get used to it.'

I put the paste I had prepared into a small silver bowl. I started on the red one. And now inexplicably Nikhil hit a loquacious streak.

'You know, I don't remember her face at all now.'

'Why?'

'I don't know. Sometimes, quite rarely, I dream of her. I feel her near me. I know by her feel that it is her. But I don't remember her face.'

He held up the portrait and stared at it solemnly.

'I think all I really remember right now are from all these old photographs. Nothing more.'

I didn't know what to say. I offered the solace hesitantly.

'Maybe if you really love someone you only need to feel them, not see them.'

He looked at me as if he saw me for the first time.

'Do you read books?'

'Not much. Not as much as I would like to.'

'You have too much work to do to get any reading done. So many servants and still the bride gets no respite. These are the best days of your life. You must get to savour them. I don't understand these people.'

'It's okay.'

I had bent closer to my work, suddenly aware this conversation must appear unseemly.

'Do you read in English?'

'I try a little. I'm not fluent at it.'

'The books in English are about how the world is. They open up our minds. You must read them.'

'So those novels are all yours?'

'Do you mean those on the shelves along the downstairs passage? Yes. If you like, I could give you a few simple ones first and then you can move on to the more challenging ones.'

'That would be nice.'

I smiled at him. He smiled back. There was soft light in his eyes. He looked so different from the silent stranger he had been so far.

✦

'Bula, these are for you,' Nikhil held out two hardbound books as he came into the dining hall for breakfast one morning: *Collections of short stories by O. Henry and Saki.*

'Why do you call her that? You must call her Bou-di,' my mother-in-law snapped.

'She is much younger than me, Ranga Ma. Bou-di is somehow not right for someone so young.'

My mother-in-law pursed her lips. Normally her word was law in the household. Only Tarapada Babu and Nikhil did as they pleased. She didn't like that but was unable to exert her will over either of them.

Sometime back I had lent Nikhil my prized copy of 'A Passage to India' quite surprised he hadn't read it yet. It had been a college text book. On its front page I had written 'Bula' followed by a star. The Bula who had finished writing her name with a flourish and with starry dreams in her eyes back then was now just a distant memory.

As Nikhil opened the book he saw the writing.

'Who is Bula?'

'That's what my friends call me.'

'It's a nice name. Can I call you Bula too? Am I your friend?'

I had laughed.

Yet it felt nice to hear my name called out in that cold remote household. The rarest occasion we had any interaction at all that he called me that, I felt reassured I had a friend.

+ + +

6

Bula: 10 years

Even all these years later, I need to just close my eyes and Ashu's face swims into my awareness. He was the best friend I had growing up.

He was a quiet brooding child with black wavy hair and fair skin, translucent and delicate.

He had enrolled in my class and we walked to school together. Normally I would chatter lots and he would ask the questions. Everything he saw in Phuleshwar puzzled him.

'Who is that?' he would ask, a skein of fear throbbing in his voice.

'Oh, that. That is Shamu Pagla. He is quite mad. He will act weird. But he won't do anything; anything to harm you, I mean.'

Ashu would stare fearfully at Shamu's menacing gestures and the half-barked threats no one understood.

And once he'd stood under that tamarind tree.

'Ashu, when will you learn? Don't you know the *shakchunni* lives on this tree where the eye can't see? She will make you her slave. Now come with me.'

'Where are you taking me?'

'Do you want her to come to you when you are asleep and drink up your soul?'

'Bula, Ma will be very cross if I am late for lunch.'

'Just come and do this quick and never stand under that tree again.'

I had to drag him almost, to the small Debi temple on the edge of the Ganga. We didn't take the path next to his house as his mother wouldn't like us wandering off after school like this.

'Now fall at the Debi's feet and ask her to fight off the shakchunni for you.'

I ran to the last step on the Ganga and using a folded leaf for a bowl got some of its magical waters.

'Here, sprinkle Ganga jal all over you. Now the shakchunni can't harm you.'

I taught him how to smash raw mangoes purloined from the extensive orchards on their grounds and mix it with salt, sugar, chilly and just a drizzle of mustard oil to make that tasty chutney. I taught him who had the best lemon drops and bull's eyes among the four sweet stalls on our way home from school. Mostly I had to defend him from the wise-asses at school who found much mirth in his city-bred shyness, gullibility and oil-slicked hair.

✦ ✦ ✦

7

Bula: 22 years

The newborn's wail rent the air.

'Oh, Ma! It's a beautiful girl. Congratulations, Ranga Ma, you have a bonny granddaughter,' the wizened old midwife cackled.

'What else would it be?' spat out my mother-in-law. 'She has always been unpropitious.'

The room was dark and a posse of women flitted in and out. The pain had been so intense and consuming that I had not noticed anything, felt neither heat nor cold. When it stopped I felt a sense of calm and peace. Exhausted, my eyelids shut and I almost drifted into sleep. Someone thrust something into my arms. It was the baby swathed in soft cotton rags.

My first thought was – what is this?

She was blotchy pink. She had sparse brown hair and surprisingly long nails at the ends of fingers so tiny they seemed unreal. When it was time to feed her, they discovered I didn't have any milk. One of the undermaids said she knew someone who could be a wet nurse. She was dispatched to conduct the negotiations.

When I finally found the space to fall asleep, a wry thought hit me. I have another human being to fend for now.

I had no idea how tough the going could be until I tried coping with the baby, my dwindling energy reserves and the increasing responsibilities that were thrust on me. Fortunately for me, the maids in the household looked at me as one of their own and they helped the most they could, even forcing me to eat and drink in the afternoons, little things they would stash away from the kitchen for me.

The pregnancy had kept me distracted. But when the baby woke me up in the middle of the night now, I stayed awake all through acutely aware of the horror of my marital situation. And the most terrifying part was that I could see no glimmer of hope or respite.

My happiest times were when I had a few minutes with the baby and could enjoy her presence.

✦

Nikhil was going past my door and happened to look in. I was on the mat on the floor playing with the baby. She was called Debjani, Deetu in short. He came to the doorway to greet me and then stood against the doorpost watching.

'She is a very beautiful baby.'

I smiled a tired, thin smile.

'You look unwell, Bula. Are you getting enough rest?'

'I'm fine.'

'I think you need to eat well and take better care of yourself.'

'It's nothing really. The baby keeps me awake some nights. I guess that's all.'

He began stopping by. One day I asked him if he would like to hold the baby. He wanted to but was afraid he would hurt her. I made him sit on the bed and softly placed the baby in his arms. He stared at her for a long time, holding her very awkwardly.

'She looks like you.'

'You think so?'

'Absolutely.'

'Nikhil, you look so nice and happy with the baby. I think you should have one of your own.'

'Why? So you don't need to share yours with me?'

'No, silly! I think you need to have a happy family of your own: a nice loving wife and your own children to dote on.'

'I'm not sure I will find a nice loving wife.'

'You surely would have met someone by now.'

He turned away. I knew I had said something improper. It made me cautious, uneasy. But he did reply.

'I did. Unfortunately, she is married.'

'Really? That's tragic. Why didn't you tell her before she did?'

There was fleeting pain in his eyes but he managed a smile.

'I only realised my feelings far too late.'

'So what will you do now?'

The baby was handed to me gently as he stood up to go. There was something of a sigh in his words.

'Nothing. Just get on with my life.'

'I sometimes worry about you, Nikhil. That is why when I see you I wish you would marry and start your own family to fill your life up.'

'Does marriage really fill anyone's life? Has yours been filled?'

I kept silent.

In time Nikhil developed ease with the baby. I would watch him play with her, enjoying the experience. He would seem carefree and less reserved somehow.

'She seems to recognise me.'

'She does. You are the only member of the household who handles her and plays with her, apart from the maids.'

'Her father doesn't? What about Ranga Ma?'

I looked away. Fortunately, Nikhil let that pass. When Deetu began to speak she would call him Neek and later, Nikhil.

'No, baby. Say Kaku.'

'Let her be, Bula. No one else calls me that and it would just confuse her. It doesn't matter to me what she calls me as long as she does.'

✦ ✦ ✦

8

Bula: 24 years

Almost three years of being "married" and still nothing in that household budged a little to make place for me. My mother-in-law continued fixing tight rosters for my daily workload. My father-in-law now and then showered an affectionate though distant smile or word. I didn't grudge that. I knew but for him, I'd be far worse off. And Aukhoy Babu did not do a thing that could clear my initial assessment of him.

The wastrel as a creed was a fairly accepted member of the society around us. In those days with scarce jobs and larger family units that found place to feed and care for everyone under the roof, the phenomenon was not quite uncommon. Just that I had come to expect some form of conviction or even common sense from practically everybody. It was of course a myth, but I imagined that those far richer with greater access to knowledge and resources would be far greater human beings as well. I simply found nothing in Aukhoy Babu to qualify him to the race.

Initially I reacted to how his public disdain for me and his careful distancing was expressed and perceived. Everybody seemed to think it was the appropriate counterfoil for private warmth. It gave him the perfect excuse to be a boor. And it bothered me. Closer acquaintance with his violence cured me soon enough. I was just happy for every moment that kept him away.

Not that wife bashing was unusual for those times either. Just that it felt extremely bleak in the absence of any warmth that could count as compensation. In all that time his only words to me always began with a rude: 'Bring me...' a cup of tea or a shirt or a towel or whatever he wanted at that moment.

✦

I was in the kitchen. A maid came in to tell me:

'Bou-di, Nikhil Dada Babu is calling you, in the dining room.'

I went to the first floor dining hall. Nikhil was alone with a cup of tea. For the first time, he was wearing formal black pants and not his jeans. He still wore his white shirt, the only colour I had seen him wear. His hair was glossy from the shower. He had shaved and I could smell his cologne even as I entered the room. He looked forbidding this morning. The tone in which he spoke was remote too.

'I need a favour. This button on my cuff has just come off. I have an important meeting and I don't have the time. Do you think you could fix it?'

'I'll get the needle box.'

When I returned, he had been given a plate of buttered toast. He placed his left forearm on the table, stretched towards me and I took the button from him to sew on. We sat in silence and while I worked, he ate hurriedly. As I bent my head and stitched, his cologne enveloped me stronger still. I had finished and leaned forward and bit off the rest of the thread with my teeth. I examined the other side. The button looked fine. I buttoned his cuff for him. He drew his wrist towards himself and examined the button. He looked at me, still removed and unsmiling.

'Thanks.'

That evening, Nikhil stopped outside my door and called my name. He held out a thin brown paper bag.

'What is this?'

'I had been to a bookstore. I got you something.'

I reached in and drew out a book called *Love Story*.

'I thought you may like it.'

'Thanks!'

I looked at him genuinely surprised and pleased at the gift. He paused, studying me, but his eyes were still shuttered, distant.

✦

When I woke up in the morning I felt very weak. Aukhoy Babu was away at Belur for a couple of days. I needed a glass of water. I called out to Debjani and asked her to hand me the covered glass that was on the bedside table.

'It's there, so near you,' she pointed. 'Why can't you take it yourself?'

'Baby, I am feeling very weak! I can't reach it.'

'Then? Will you die?'

An undermaid came to clean the rooms. I bid her to call Sraboni, who was a very distant relative and stayed in this household, helping out.

'Sraboni, I am feeling very ill. Will you take Deetu down with you and take care of her for today?

'Bou-di, you look sick. Shall I call Ranga Ma?'

I didn't want to disturb my mother-in-law.

'If I sleep a little I think I'll be fine. Don't worry her needlessly.'

I was swept away in a grey haze almost as soon as my head touched the pillow.

'Kishore-da!' I heard a voice call out in the adjoining outer room. I sat up with a start. I must tell him Aukhoy Babu is not here, I felt. I made it to the door between the rooms.

It was Nikhil.

'Bula, where is...' he began. Then his eyes widened. 'Are you alright?'

I held the door post for support and suddenly my legs became wobbly and my mind went blank.

He had grabbed me before I could collapse and held me unsure what to do next. My eyes flickered open and focused with some difficulty on a very worried looking Nikhil.

'Bula, what's wrong?'

I tried to speak but words abandoned me.

'You are burning up. I'll have to send for a doctor. Be here with you in a minute, okay?

He came back and sat beside me on the bed. Now he fussed with the bedclothes: covering me with a clean sheet, moving a pillow out of the way and propping a bolster next to me.

In a while the doctor came in with Akhil and Sraboni.

'What's the matter?' the doctor asked.

'I think it's very high fever,' Nikhil answered.

'Yes, there is some sort of flu in the air. Let me see.'

The doctor confirmed his snap diagnosis. He left a lot of scary-looking capsules with Nikhil and precise diet instructions.

My mother-in-law had been invited to a first rice ceremony in her extended family. She came in to see me on her way out all dressed up, her heavy silk rustling and her beauty products filling the room with perfume.

'So, Nikhil, what happened?'

'The doctor thinks it is influenza, Ranga Ma.'

'Tell Sujoya when to give her the medicines. You don't sit here. It may be contagious. Just go off to office soon. And eat something before you go.'

'Thanks, I will, Ranga Ma.'

'Well, see you tomorrow in the evening then. I must be off.'

I flitted between sleep and waking that whole day. Death warmed up, I was later told that feeling was called. That raw gloom and floating when nothing really feels right. Whenever I opened my eyes, they were drawn towards the silhouette of Nikhil sitting quietly on a chair beside my bed, reading his book. Somehow having him there filled me with a sense of peace. He'd raise his head and ask me:

'Do you want something to eat?'

I'd shake my head and in a little while sleep would claim me again.

The room was fully dark. Someone spoke to me trying to wake me up. I opened my eyes feeling both disjointed and languorous.

'It is almost ten in the night now, Bula. Please wake up and eat something. I'm sorry, I have to go too. Anyway Sujoya is bringing you some toast and soup. I'll give her the medicines. She will be with you tonight. I'll be back in the morning.'

I then realised that his hand still lay cupping my cheek. It was the first gesture of kindness I'd been shown in a long time. It stirred up forgotten feelings within me. I could feel tears pricking my eyelids.

'Okay. Thank you.' I whispered.

Soon Sujoya came in and he was gone.

✦ ✦ ✦

9

Bula: 25 years

All the family businesses were closed on Sundays. Late every Saturday night, Nikhil would send up three hardbound registers which would lay on the dresser by Aukhoy Babu's room door. They contained detailed accounts of the business transacted over the week.

Aukhoy Babu rarely even glanced at them. His major pastime lately had been accompanying this band of unoccupied aging men who had formed a bhajan group. Their singing was raucous. What they patently lacked in musical talent they sought to make up for in volume and fervour. The whole band was invited in turns to various households and small temples. He saw himself mainly in the role of a band manager: sat a little apart from the singers, rapt in devotion and the decidedly unmusical rendition.

Late one Monday morning, Nikhil himself came by to collect the registers. That day, as if impelled by some strange curiosity I had taken all these registers and as they lay open across the mat I sat cross-legged before them and read them through. I tried to make sense of the figures and the correlations between them: such as the sharp jump in the sales of Gobindo bhog rice in all our outlets and the wedding season just gone by.

When Nikhil spoke, I started guiltily.

'I was just looking...' I began lamely.

He stood quietly for a while.

'It is your right. As a member of this family.' Then he added: 'Bula, could you look at the accounts with me from time to time? Kishore-da doesn't. It would be nice to have someone within the family also involved.'

How he managed to work this element out I did not know. My mother-in-law had consented. Since then, every Sunday after breakfast I went down to the smaller drawing room which no one used. We sat at that imposing teak desk, Nikhil and I, and deciphered the accounts together. I knew nothing of what was expected of me. But I had a very patient teacher. He explained things which I couldn't understand and answered my stupidest questions with serious intent. He encouraged me to rework some of the calculations so that I soon became a reliable source to cross check the totals. This task also provided me a welcome diversion and purpose apart from the drudgery of the household work. I began to enjoy working with the figures and indulging in hypothetical forecasts for the immediate future of the business. But most of all, I had developed a functional relationship with another adult and that, I had not had since I entered this house.

Some weeks later, we both reached to turn the page together and as our fingers touched I jerked mine away jumpily. It slid against the silvered edges of the page and an angry red slash stood brilliant across the length of my finger.

'What's this?' he seized my finger to examine it better. 'It's cut badly.'

'It's just a scratch,' I countered.

He thrust his chair back and strode out of the room. I could hear him calling out. In a while h came in with the first aid box.

'Why are you yelling?' My mother-in-law followed her in, asking. 'Oh, it's you.'

Nikhil found the cotton and the spirit and mopped up the few droplets of blood I thought he was making an unnecessary fuss over. For once my mother-in-law and I were in agreement.

'Womenfolk have to tolerate a lot worse than this. They can't afford to fuss over nothing. What's the need for all this?'

'Ranga Ma, even a minor cut can get infected. It's better to treat it immediately.'

The spirit stung and my fingers would flinch and curl; so he held it firm throughout his ministrations.

✦

The realisation that I was pregnant again had been a nasty shock to me. Our conjugal ties had been non-existent lately.

This baby was named Geetanjali. She was a little sickly and as demanding as Debjani was cheerful. She had a feisty spirit and in her I saw a lot of what I had once been. This time I could feed the baby. It wasn't a task I was overjoyed to do. I had marshalled the old wet nurse again to share my duties. But it felt nice to hold the little scrawny thing to my breast and watch her quietly fall asleep, sated.

When I was heavily pregnant with Geetu I began to have a little issue with my blood pressure. I had been feeling a little dizzy all afternoon. I struggled to sit up by evening. Suddenly my mother-in-law walked in.

'Come to Kishore's room,' she commanded.

I waddled my way there. She sat next to Aukhoy Babu on the bed. I found my way to a chair and sank in.

'You know the circumstances of your marriage better than anybody.' It was almost spat out. 'Kishore only married you because he wanted to appease his father and the world to see him as a normal householder. You were chosen because you were poor and could appreciate the honour done to you. However, you have not been able to deter him from his true calling. My son now chooses to renounce the world. He has my blessings. I know there is greatness in him. And perhaps as a monk he will realise himself. But it seems as a householder he can only do so if his wife consents. In writing. So I demand that you free him from all obligations to you immediately.'

I looked down. I said mildly:

'He has never had any obligations towards me.'

'That may have to do more with what you are than him. Now sign this letter. And yes, you cannot let your father-in-law know any of this. As he's grown older he has become extremely strong-willed and doesn't hesitate to harm even his own son.'

An unknown source of strength gave me the courage to voice a demand of my own. There are moments no one is immune to blackmail.

'Before I sign anything that permanent I would also like to have legal and binding papers that would safeguard me and my girls. This is actually the dissolution of a marriage. Where will we go then?'

That seemed to flummox the two of them. I went on.

'I need the guarantee that we can stay on here as we always have, even in the event of Baba's demise. And perhaps as a monk that is a given, yet I would also need the assurance that never again in his life will he come anywhere near me or in any way expect me to behave as his wife.'

'He is not the least bit interested in you. Haven't you understood that by now?'

'And yet he has already fathered two children.... I would still prefer to have all these in writing.'

'Very well. He will never come near you again.'

And with those simple words I felt a sense of great liberation. I looked him in the eye and said with immense joy.

'You have no obligation towards me. You will not come near me again. You have my consent to renounce me.'

The next morning the servants began moving all his things downstairs. Aukhoy Babu moved into a room in what used to be his parent's suite on the ground floor, beside the room his mother now occupied. And he never stepped onto the second floor again. That fact purchased me a huge sense of relief.

Of course the stamped paper that my signature was taken on the following day in return for a badly worded document that assured shelter for my girls and me, would not hold water in any court. It still provided immense relief to me and proved a watershed event in my life.

✦

I am not sure whether it was due to the pressure problems, but Geetu was born a month before she was expected. Nikhil's wedding had been fixed for that time. My mother-in-law had pressurised him to marry Reba, both beautiful and rich, who she had hand-picked from among those recommended by her large family circle. I was unable to attend the wedding in my condition. I was told it was beautiful and elegant, but limited to only a small number of family members and friends.

From the beginning my mother-in-law was deferential to the new bride. The beautiful Reba would spend all her time in her room in the east wing, rarely involving herself in any household matter. She subscribed to a lot of film magazines and absorbed herself fully in the world of movie stars and their peccadilloes. The household tailor who came once every month would be pressed into creating ornate blouses for her with net, lace, sequin, bead and ruche embellishments.

✦

All our rooms had doors on two opposite sides. One led to the narrow passage that over looked the large square courtyard. The other led to a wide verandah that skirted the house on each floor. After Aukhoy Babu moved downstairs, I began using the verandah freely. On cooler days, I would spend precious moments of my freer afternoons reading in a comfortable cane chair placed just outside my door. A gardener had brought in many beautiful potted plants all along our verandah and it was a cool verdurous hideaway.

Reba's father had gifted her a stereo system and she played sentimental songs on unrequited love all day so loud that its sounds wafted through the household. On evenings when I sat down with a cup of tea, sometimes Reba would come and sit with me. My mother-in-law had made sure Reba was filled in on my background and Reba would patronise me, as one would a social inferior one pities immensely; if it wasn't my impoverished background it was the sad demeaning fact that I had been relinquished by my husband. That didn't bother me much. I had been in that household too long to care anymore. Just the joy of not being subject to Aukhoy Babu's proximity was a cause for unbridled joy.

Over time I realised that Reba rarely stayed in the house. Her family and immense friend circle always had many weddings and social functions that she would go away weeks for. That air of loneliness that I sensed around Nikhil had only deepened with his marriage. I felt a twinge of pain that someone as special as Nikhil had been yoked for life to someone who seemed preoccupied, in a sense unappreciative and uncaring.

✦ ✦ ✦

10

Bula: 26 years

Sraboni came to my room late one evening and said, 'Dada Babu is calling you.'

'Aukhoy Babu?'

'Yes. In Ranga Ma's Room.'

This was unprecedented and I tried to shake of that sense of alarm. As I stepped off the last stair I could hear a loud commotion. I approached my mother-in-law's room apprehensively. Summons from Aukhoy Babu were now part of a much forgotten history.

'Sulochona Debi, it's quite serious...' Aukhoy Babu began faintly blubbering.

'Why are you sounding apologetic, Kishore? Scold her and demand that she return it at once.' My mother-in-law shouted.

'What happened?' I ventured to ask.

'What happened? Look at her, all innocence and sweetness. You have stolen my gold chain!'

'What? Me?'

'Don't try your histrionics on me. When you come from a poverty-ridden home, will you be able to resist a fifteen sovereign gold chain?'

'Ma, it may be that she didn't mean it like that.'

Part of the indoctrination he was currently undergoing was of being the better man. I'd noticed it at mealtimes often too.

'Shut up, Kishore. What else can you mean if you steal my gold chain? Came into my room with the flimsiest of questions. Do you want the *pabda* in mustard paste? Then she saw it lying there and just took it.'

'I didn't steal anything. It may have been misplaced. Someone else may have taken it....'

'No servant here will dare touch my things. And what better are you than a maid here, huh? Just because my idiot son once made the mistake of marrying you.'

'Sulochona Debi, return it. Ma will forgive you.'

Just then Sujoya entered with the chain.

'Found it, Ranga Ma. It was on the shelf by the wash basin. You must have taken it off when you were washing your face.'

'Ohhh! Thank god it is safe.'

I turned and ran from the room, almost colliding with Nikhil at the doorway.

I ran up the stairs as fast as my feet would carry me, feeling my heart would burst. And on to the furthest point in the terrace behind the water tank and standing there in the dark, huge dry sobs racking my body. I didn't have the leisure to commiserate with the events for long. I needed to go down to pitch in with the dinner preparations. A figure stood by the side, waiting. It was Nikhil. I didn't want to move. I stole the dare of staying as long as I could. There was a sense of comfort even if unspoken in that dark dank spot on the terrace. Then I knew, I simply had to tear myself away.

'Bula...'

I couldn't find the voice to reply.

'Please forgive us all! We are all heartless freaks with too much money on our minds.'

'Please don't apologise. To me...'

'Bula, leave Kishore-da and go away from here.'

His voice was raspy and tortured. I looked up at him sharply, shocked.

'I promise I will send you and the girls enough money every month. For as long as I live. You don't have to take this kind of nonsense.'

'I have nowhere to go.'

'Go back to your mother.'

'A public admission of a failed marriage would kill her.'

He turned away from me with an exclamation and walked away to a far wall. Then without a word, he turned on his heel and left. I stood there with strange emotions growing in me, feeling suddenly orphaned in his absence.

✦

A tragedy befell the household. Tarapada Babu had fallen down unconscious in the bathroom. He was discovered more than an hour later with a very feeble pulse, bleeding from an open wound where his head had hit a tap. He had suffered a cerebral stroke. He was admitted to a renowned hospital and given the best medical attention. He survived for two weeks aided by machines. And then, passed away.

Nikhil, Akhil, Aukhoy Babu and his mother went a month later to perform the final offerings of *til* for the peace of his soul at Gaya. From there the brothers were to return home while Aukhoy Babu and his mother would go onward for a month's stay at Benaras.

The house seemed so rambling and formidable with everyone away. By now the twins and the kids were all asleep. The servants had all left the main building and to go on to their quarters. After supervising all the locks and double checking the bolts and bars, I was about to go up to my room. There was a gentle tap at the main door.

'Who is it?' I called out.

'It's me. Nikhil.'

I realised then how much I had missed having him around. I fumbled with the bars hating every second's delay in flinging open the doors.

Nikhil wore his usual jeans with a kurta crumpled by the journey. A rough grey shawl hung around his shoulders. His hair had grown back stubbly. His angular features looked gaunt as he stood unsmiling before me.

Every fibre in my body yearned to fling myself into his arms and welcome his homecoming. I stood stone still registering that I had never felt these emotions for any other human being.

Akhil came up carrying the bags.

'What's the matter? Why aren't you going inside?'

I stepped aside to let them pass. Akhil just dropped the bags there. I reached out and took the pot of Ganga jal from Nikhil and set it down on the table against the wall.

'Will you both bathe now? What will you eat?'

'Bou-di I ate a lot of junk on the train. I'm off to sleep. Bath-*wath* in the morning,' Akhil replied.

'Can Sraboni heat me a little water?'

'Sraboni is sleeping with the kids. I'll heat it.'

'I don't want you to bother. I'll just bathe in cold water.'

'In this weather? At this time of the night? Go get your things, I'll get the water. And what would you like to eat?'

'Don't bother with food.'

We had large copper basins in which bath water was heated through the day on wood fires. Now I filled one and set it on the gas to heat. Then I took it to the bathroom, split it between two buckets and began topping them both with tap water, dipping my fingers in the water I made sure it was warm. By the time I was done, Nikhil was at the bathroom door.

Each night after dinner was done the leftover food was given away to the servants to take with them and to feed the strays. There was nothing left of our sparse dinner to give Nikhil. The only option was to rustle up some simple meal, and the chosen one was *rooti-s* with potatoes. I made very thin puffy rooti-s and coated them with a dollop of ghee. He had finished his bath and had stopped outside the kitchen door, almost uncertain where to go next.

His head glistened with water and his kurta clung to wet patches on his skin.

'You will catch a cold,' I exclaimed.

I took the towel from his hands.

'Please bend down a little?' I requested and silently, dutifully he stooped.

What I could get of the moisture on his head I wiped away. I found his shawl still warm and fragrant from his body, hung on a peg in the bathroom and brought it to drape around him. I led him to the room next to the kitchen where all the womenfolk ate. We sat on low wooden platforms and now I set one down and placed the plate before it. He sat down but did not touch his food.

'I'm not hungry.'

I was at that cavernous fridge at the far end of the room looking for sweets. There was a pot of *rosogollas* and I was serving a couple on to a bowl. I came and sat down on the floor beside him.

I took a piece of the rooti and potatoes and held it to his mouth. He ate it. We sat in perfect silence, me feeding him as if he were a small boy in need of comfort. At the end of the meal, I cut each rosogolla into half and held each piece to his mouth with a spoon. A little syrup trickled down the side of his mouth. I reached out and wiped it away.

The plates needed to be cleaned and so I went into the kitchen to wash up by the sink. He followed me in wordlessly and stood by while I worked.

I wanted to talk to him, ask him questions about his trip but was afraid of breaking this cocoon of intimate silence that bound us together. I switched off the kitchen lights and bolted the door on the outside. He still stood outside the kitchen while I walked away. I turned the end of the passage and went towards the stairs in the middle of the other side.

'Will you stay with me tonight?' he'd spoken extremely low but I had heard him.

I stopped. I didn't dare turn around. My mind froze. There was no way I was supposed to be alone with Nikhil, ever; but definitely never through the night. And yet there was nothing

I wanted to do more than to be with him. A spark of defiance lit up in me. I had done what everyone else had demanded for far too long. What did I get in return? When would I find my peace? I felt tired of denying myself. I felt tired of loneliness and misery.

I turned around to face him. We stood in that dim light of the sleeping household with a vast ocean between us. Numerous comments and misgivings on propriety, decency and overstepping boundaries clamoured unspoken in that space. What mattered despite it all were the assertions of my heart and the haunting plea in his eyes.

Nikhil walked to where I stood, rooted, at the foot of the stairs. He went past me and I followed him. He went into his study, beside the room Aukhoy Babu used to occupy. There was a connecting door between the two now barred with heavy book shelves on this side and a wardrobe on the other.

In the warm glow of the intimate yellow bulb, his room seemed to glow. It was huge and airy, with lots of tall windows opening out onto the greenery outside. They had pale blue cotton curtains. Against a wall there was a narrow bed with pure white bedclothes. The walls were all completely lined with bookshelves. At a far corner there was a writing table.

He led me to an upholstered chair, covered in deep green leather. He himself sat on a lounge chair with a padded headrest. He brought his feet up, picked up a book from the exaggeratedly long armrest and finding his page, began to read.

I sat in silence for a while. Then I walked up to the bookshelves and read the book titles trying to see whether I could find reading material too. I chose an orange paperback called 'The Catcher in the Rye'. Its title intrigued me. When I came back to my chair, he went to the bed, stooped and pulled out from under it a foot rest also upholstered in the same green. As I sat, he adjusted the foot rest and reached out a hand to check what book I had chosen. Returning it wordlessly he went back to his reading.

He was absorbed in the book, at peace with this silence and the world in general. I found out pretty soon that the book I had picked was American. The vernacular was strange and peppered with a slang I was not conversant with. The protagonist is a teenage boy who I found difficult to identify with just then. My mind wandered. I would steal glances at Nikhil over the edge of my page.

By around three in the morning he fell asleep. His head rested at ease against the back of his chair. The book lay loosely in fingers weakened by sleep. I sat almost still watching him breathe in and out. Then I carefully took the book, inserted his bookmark and set it down. As I tucked the blanket around his shoulders his eyes fluttered open and he looked at me with unseeing unsmiling eyes. He was soon fast asleep again.

I sat through the night simply revelling in the joy of being with Nikhil. As I looked at his sleeping form I realised with a slowly dawning clarity what he had come to mean to me. My mind grappled with the acceptance of this reality which I had pushed to the farthest corner of my subconscious for too long now. I felt liberated from a huge burden. I felt ecstatic that I had a reason to live.

I spent the night keeping a vigil over my newly discovered secret and this man who scripted it.

As dawn broke and the window panes grew lighter my magical night was over. Yet, I felt hopeful and immensely happy. I stood by Nikhil's chair in silence. Then I bent and touched my fingertips to his forehead in a stolen caress and went back to my room before the household came awake.

✦ ✦ ✦

11

Bula: 26 years

Late Sunday morning. We had been working for a while. Nikhil suggested we take a break. He went and flung himself on the day bed and stared up at the ceiling grimly. I turned around in my chair and watched him as he lay there looking exhausted.

'Come sit here beside me.' He tapped the edge of the bed.

We sat in comfortable silence for a while. Then he spoke up:

'Bula, does it bother you that you are in a bad marriage? I think having to live and deal with Reba is the unhappiest thing I have had to put up with.'

On the rare occasion that we spoke or worked together, we had the greatest of ease, even warm companionship. Yet, the very overt reticence in Nikhil's nature made me uncomfortable when he decided to just speak out.

'Maybe it takes more time for some marriages to get better.'

'If time is all it takes, yours would have been great by now.'

'Aukhoy Babu has mostly been kind.'

'Kind? Rubbish! Don't give me that guff. He has just abused you physically, mentally and emotionally all these years.'

'By nature he is a weaker person.'

'So weak that he forgets he has a beautiful warm-blooded wife to take care of? Come on. Has he even been in your bed five times in these past five years?'

I hung my head down.

'Shit! I'm sorry I said that. Forgive me.'

He held the ball of fingers my hands were clasped into, briefly.

'You are someone I understand, Bula. When I look at you I see the kind of person any man would be grateful to have in his life. And someone undeserving and useless like Kishore-da is lucky enough to have you. Yet all he does is abuse and belittle you at every step. And then I see Reba. I try so hard to form a bond with her, create a sense of togetherness and build a sustainable relationship. And she is just wrapped up in herself, she can't see the world beyond her immediate needs and desire for things. People, relationships, emotions or any higher aspirations are just beyond her. I think anybody who is forced to partner her is just doomed to a life of misery.'

I sat silent.

'Why aren't you saying anything?'

'I can't think of anything to say.'

'You are angry about what I said regarding Kishore-da, aren't you?'

'No. Can we get back to work?'

'I don't believe you.'

'Nikhil, let's get back to work.'

'Bula...'

He said no more, just continued lying on the bed staring up at the ceiling. In a while I spoke up.

'About Aukhoy Babu...I am grateful that he married me. Before that I was being supported by my uncle, as charity. When he married me, he gave me an acceptable toehold in the world. I had my own place in society.'

'That was incidental, Bula. Apart from that, what did he give you?'

'I think maybe he is not capable of giving any more.'

'That cannot be enough. Marrying you and forgetting all about the woman he married cannot be enough. I go through it with Reba all the time that she is wrapped up in her parties and festivities. It makes no sense to live on the fringes of someone's life. How can it be enough for you, Bula?'

'Sometimes, very different people get married. They don't understand how different until it is too late. They make the most of their reality, taking solace where they find it. He found it in his devotion to God....'

'And you?'

I thought it over very carefully.

'I find solace in the positive things in my life and the people around me, the kids, my work, you...'

He sprang from the bed and was on his feet, his eyes shining dangerously.

'What is wrong with you? Can't you see I am also just like Kishore-da? I come to you only in my time of need and then withdraw, uncaring what your needs may be. Hasn't it happened to you time and again? Isn't it true?'

'What do you want from me, Nikhil?' I asked in a quiet voice.

'Oh God!'

He sank back on the bed low, holding his head.

'I want nothing from you. I think I am going mad to even by talking like this.'

We sat like that side by side, divided by multitudes of emotions neither had much of a hold over. Slowly I reached out and ran my fingers through his hair. He didn't move away. So I moved closer tentatively and put an arm around him.

'I'm sorry,' I said.

'For what?'

'That you are going through so much.'

'Heal me, Bula. Save me.'

I held him close, resting my cheek against his hair. I prayed he find the peace which this godforsaken situation was denying him.

✦

The kids were playing on the grass with Sraboni and Sujoya. I sat on a garden bench a little way off, enjoying the scene and retreating into my own thoughts in turns. A car drove into the covered driveway. I turned. It was Nikhil. He came up to where all of us were.

'How come you are here today?'

With Ma and Aukhoy Babu still away having extended their sojourn in Varanasi, there was a sense of peace and calm in the household, and the freedom it afforded me was unique and sweet. For the first time I was enjoying living in this house. I didn't tell him that.

'All the food is already cooked. I really have little work pending. So I decided to make the most of it. I've chosen the garden to relax in and watch the kids play.'

'Good. I know you need the break.'

'You are home awfully early.'

'I had work at a government office fairly close by. I didn't feel like going all the way back to office, so I decided to come back to...come home instead.'

He sat down beside me. Both of us watched the kids frolic.

'Would you like tea or something?'

'No, I'm fine.'

On impulse I leaned over and unbuttoned his cuffs and folded his sleeves back up to his elbows. I even undid the top button on his shirt front. I brushed his collar down.

'There, now you look a lot relaxed.'

There was that ease and warmth in his eyes as he looked at me.

'Thanks!'

He stretched his legs out and tapped his shod feet against each other.

The shouts and the laughter of the kids as they played formed the backdrop to our togetherness. The sun sank lower. The light changed. We were all caught in a strange suffuse haze. I recall my mother had once called this light "*godhuli*" – the dust of the gods or was it of the cows coming home.... It was a pink-golden glow and made everything it touched magical. I turned to look at Nikhil. He seemed radiant, his face looking heartbreakingly handsome and vulnerable at the same time. I knew I was staring but I couldn't tear my eyes away. He felt my gaze upon him and turned towards me enquiringly. I still couldn't turn away. I think he saw something in my eyes and in response I saw his eyes darken. My eyes searched his face; scanned every feature for the smallest detail to be imprinted on my soul forever. We sat looking at each other, wishing there was a way out, a way to speak or lighten the moment and both were unable to find it.

Almost involuntarily two fingers reached out and touched my hair wonderingly. He whispered:

'Bula, you look so beautiful!'

I was still spellbound. I opened my mouth to speak and couldn't. I simply managed to breathe his name.

'Nikhil...'

'Nikhil!' Deetu ran and flung herself into his lap. 'Come play with me.'

I got up then and went to pick up Geetu as she had wandered too close to a rose bush.

✦ ✦ ✦

12

Bula: 14 years

We were around fourteen, Ashu and I. My mother was over at a much pregnant neighbour's house cleaning and cooking. She was incredibly hard working and charitable by nature. Often people gave her some food or grains to be taken away and that helped us subsist. I remember we were sitting on my bed playing snakes and ladders. The board had been a gift from an uncle and was made of cardboard with a gaudily printed paper pattern. The brightly coloured snakes stood out their maws wide open menacingly. I climbed this ladder that took me just three counts away from the winning point and past the last snake.

'You cheated,' Ashu accused me.

'No. I got that ladder fair and square,' I protested.

He threw himself on me and mock punched me. I sank into the pillows laughing. And suddenly I was aware that I lay trapped under his body that seemed somehow so light and enchanted. His face hovered above mine. His voice had turned by then and now carried a timbre that I felt throbbed with an intensity.

'Bula, I love you! Did you know that?' he said very slowly, earnestly.

'Of course, you idiot. I love you, too,' I said laughing.

'Not like that, Bula. Like I want to marry you. Like I never want to live a single day without you by my side. Like you are my woman, Bula. Only mine.'

I stared into the deep lights of his eyes. I had loved him like that almost since the day I met him. I had taken care of him all along and given him my complete companionship only because of how much I loved him. The intensity of what I felt frightened me.

We looked gravely into each other's faces, memorising each detail. His head bent and his lips were on mine. Our bodies ground together as if nothing mattered more in the world than getting as close as possible to each other.

✦ ✦ ✦

13

Bula: 26 years

Only on extremely rare occasions did the household empty out completely. It was a Sunday when it unexpectedly did. I went down to the drawing room as usual. Nikhil came in a little late. His hair was tousled. There was a wild light in his eyes. He didn't come much past the doorway, but stopped and stared at me.

The air between us crackled. In his eyes I read longing and efforts at restraint. I wondered what he saw in mine.

'What's the matter?' I asked as coolly as I could muster.

'Nothing,' he replied brusquely.

He stood taut with uncertainty, almost angrily.

'Would it help to know that I too feel the same way?'

'It's impossible!' he bit out.

'Okay. So, it's impossible.' I turned back to the open books.

He grabbed me by my upper arm, so hard that later I realised he had bruised me.

'What do you feel?' he demanded to know.

I bowed my head, my knees unsteady, almost unable to frame my thoughts in words. It came out simply.

'I love you, Nikhil!'

He dropped my arm as if it were red hot and turned away.

'And if you were honest with yourself you would know that in your own way you love me too.'

'You are Kishore-da's wife.'

'Yes, I know. That does not change anything.'

'That is the only thing that matters.

'No, it doesn't. If at any point our pathetic lives had any meaning, it was given to each other – by you and me, Nikhil. And by no one else. Not by Aukhoy Babu. Not by Reba.'

'Bula, don't!'

'Don't what? Don't stare reality in the face?'

'I...I need to go.'

He took a step towards the door.

'Don't walk out on me now, Nikhil,' it was a small tired voice. 'I...I am scared too.'

That stopped him. He turned back, unmoving, not meeting my eye.

I went up to him. It was capitulation to all that hurt and desire deep within as I rested my head against his shirt front, asking for refuge more than anything. He stood cold and frozen. Then slowly, almost unwillingly, his fingertips went to the back of my head, offering meagre respite. That was enough. I needed to see his face and the pain I saw etched there made me reach to touch. And in that touch there was longing. Almost unwittingly I raised to my toes to press my lips against his. He remained unresponsive still. Then I slowly felt them move, almost a flutter at first. Hesitantly, he kissed me back.

It was the most beautiful feeling on earth! Stunned by the enormity of what had just happened we practically sprang apart and yet drank in with wonder the realisation that the warmth and caring and comfort with each other we had always known was this, spiralling magical overwhelming love. And that this warmth translated perfectly into this new language we had just discovered to express what lay buried in us.

Acting at the same time almost hypnotically we reached out for each other. This kiss was neither soft nor hesitant. It was born of a craving both of us had suppressed for too long now. Our mouths pleaded for and demanded much more from the other. Two lonely thirsty souls finding water in the other. Our spouses, the practical sin of our actions, all notions of impropriety and obscenity faded in this need that had grown between us and refused to be denied anymore.

We touched each other; our fingers fanning over each other's skin, each pore absorbing warmth from the other. The gentle exploration turned hungrier, more urgent until we faced each other's innermost desire. And at that point, I knew there was no turning back. And I was unafraid. Only deliriously happy.

When we found this small pause of sanity to surface, he smiled a happy lazy smile.

'Let's look at the accounts in the evening. Let's go up to my study.'

In his study, Nikhil lay down on his narrow bed and drew me down on his chest. There are so many little things lovers need to say and do. This was beyond the need for food or the intrusion of any other thought. We stayed together until the first knock on the door that evening. We spent hours exploring each other. We talked about things we wanted the other to know. At times we just stayed together in silence, happy to be with each other like this, like two puppies squishing into the comfort of the other.

That evening when we went down to do the accounts together, the children and the maids were all making a racket in the courtyard. After requesting them to pipe down a couple of times Nikhil shut the door with a bang. Ever since, we did our accounts behind closed doors.

These turned into our frenzied moments of bliss. This is what I looked forward to through the dreary hours of the week. As we worked through increasingly complex data, we turned to each other with greater need. Me with a sense of wonder and awe at the man I loved while he touched me like I was fragile.

We held hands. We kissed. Our hands roved, caressing each other. This was our own little world, our secret paradise – his and mine.

✦

I had appeared at the door of his study. He was on his lounge chair, reading.

'Come with me, please.'

'Where?'

'Don't ask questions. Just come.'

'Tell me where we are going?'

'Trust me.'

He picked up his watch from the hand rest and began slipping it on.

'No. You don't need that.'

I held him by the wrist and led him upstairs to the terrace.

'The terrace? Now?'

We were out on the terrace in the face of a heavy wind laden with the promise of rain. I bolted the terrace door from the outside, lest it slam.

'Bula, we will get wet.'

Small droplets began to fall. I stretched out my palms as far as I could and looked heavenwards.

'Yes. Isn't it wonderful?'

'We'll both catch a cold. Wouldn't that be wonderful?'

'Stop being a spoilsport. Look at the sky. You can see the raindrops come down.'

He looked up and quickly looked down again.

'I think one of them got my eye.'

I rushed to him.

'Let me see.'

I gently patted his afflicted eye.

'Does it hurt?'

The rain began pelting down then.

'Okay, so we are wet. Completely. Shall we go in now?'

Water slicked back our hair. Our clothes hung heavy with water, sticking in brown patches to our skin. Raindrops beaded our faces.

'Rains have never been pleasant for me, Nikhil. Growing up beside the river, they invariably caused water-logging and slush. In extremes they brought floods. I avoid rain, have all my life. This morning when I woke up and saw the rain clouds, I had the overwhelming desire to befriend them. I have this hunger to taste more, feel more since...since you.

'And do you know why I brought you along? To overcome my fear. If you are my by my side and if we do this together, it would never again be unpleasant to me. I want to rewrite my memories, my life ahead, Nikhil with you.'

He reached out and cupped my face, reading my face like it was a book he loved. Then he leaned forward and drank the rain water from my lips.

There were the clouds, the wind, the pouring rain and just the two of us. All external realities ceased to exist. The trappings of civilisation faded. The clothes that we wore that placed us in a time within a milieu went. We could have been a couple of Neanderthals caught between rain and a primeval passion.

Our lovemaking was simple, unhurried and deep. Fully spent we lay on the terrace floor with milder raindrops washing over our fused bodies.

I shivered a little. He held me closer.

'I hope we don't catch pneumonia.'

Neither of us moved.

✦ ✦ ✦

14

Bula: 26 years

It was an elaborate Sunday meal that had been in preparation since morning. The bell metal utensils shone like dull gold. The old manservant Haradhon Kaku, I guess our household's equivalent to a butler, undertook the serving with great pride, scolding the three undermaids who fetched and poured water, clumsy in their nervousness. My mother-in-law sat at the table with her palm leaf fan, not eating but revelling in the role of the matriarch. Talks were on about what was to be done with Akhil now that he was done with his graduation.

Just then Sujoya came in ushering a gentleman who looked vaguely familiar. He was Reba's Uncle.

'Praise the Lord, Nikhil Babu! You have a baby boy.'

He still looked at the plate he was eating from.

'Is that so?'

And then he looked up and straight at me. My face had broken into a smile of genuine happiness for him.

'I hope both mother and child are doing well.'

That look was a rare moment of public intimacy that I knew stemmed from his sudden realisation that the situation we were in may not be the easiest.

However the moment was immediately lost in my mother-in-law's theatrics. She was shrieking in joy, babbling incoherently about her happiness and not omitting to mention some others who did not do their duty and persistently bore daughters.

✦

It was perhaps a month after. He was at the table. The number of registers to be monitored now had risen to seven. I was a little later than usual. The girls were supposed to attend a family function at a playmate's home. Dressing them and getting them ready to go was a struggle for me despite the fluttering help of both Sraboni and Sujoya; especially with Geetanjali.

He looked up from the books watching me shut and bolt the door. He rose as I moved closer. He held out a small maroon velvet box.

'What's this?'

'It's for you.'

I took it and opened it curiously. In it lay a simple ring with a large white stone that sparkled so furiously passionate, it could only have been a diamond. I gasped at its beauty.

'What is this for?'

'When I had to go see the boy and er...Reba, Ranga Ma gave me my mother's ring to give...her. Somehow that didn't feel right.'

He held my hand lightly, found the ring finger on my left hand and slipped it on. It was beautiful. I couldn't tear my gaze away.

'I didn't want to go. I didn't want to give her anything. So I first went into a store and spent hours until lunchtime looking for something I could give you. When I went there I told them I already had lunch and that there was important business to attend to. I stayed only as long as I had to.'

He held me close, apologetically, his chest heaving at the recollections of his actions. While we worked the ring seemed to flash with every move of my hand to turn the pages or to reach for a receipt. I kept staring at it in wonder. He caught me looking at it once and putting an arm around me, drew me close, bringing to a halt all work for a while.

The work was demanding. We took short breaks every time we finished a set. I think it was only this and each other's company that made the work tolerable. Each time we returned to the figures, it was with renewed energy.

At the end of that day's quantum of work, I pushed back my chair and held out my hand so that I could marvel at the sparkle again. Then I began removing the ring.

'Why are you doing that?'

'People will surely notice.'

'Let them. Please don't take it off. Wear it always for me.'

I could only smile. I looked at the beautiful ring as it lay in my palm, suddenly even more precious, a concrete reminder of him who was now my life. I slipped off my chain and slid the ring into it like a pendant.

'This way I can wear it forever.'

I looked down as it nestled in the hollow of my chest, close to my heart.

The days stretched arid between the interludes Sundays provided. Not that the quantum of work or responsibilities had reduced. Not that anything had altered. On rare mornings I saw Nikhil but briefly on his way out or at breakfast. Dinner time was a longer span but frozen under the glare of public interaction, I could let no sign escape. Not even a glance at him. Yet that throbbing secret music that my heart now played kept me alive, ecstatic.

There were some new contracts to be read and approved of. The lawyers had provided their own supplementary notes to simplify the legal jargon. Yet it was bewilderingly heavy reading.

'Just sign, Bula. Why are you breaking your head over it?'

'If you ask me to, there is no question of not signing. It's just that I want to understand this idiom better.'

I moved from the table and sat on the day bed with all the files, my knees steepled in front of me. I knew it would be better to just give in to Nikhil's advice. And yet I wanted to get familiar with this language and to understand its nuances; especially to cross-check whether under the guise of heavy verbiage there were some legal loopholes.

Nikhil reached out from his chair and ran a finger over my right foot. I quickly pulled my feet away.

'What happened?'

'Nikhil, don't touch my feet.'

'Why?'

'Nobody should touch my feet. And least of all, you....'

'Why are your feet off limits?'

'They are dirty, Nikhil. Besides you hold a place of tremendous respect in my life.'

'Can I touch you anywhere else?'

'Yes.'

'But not your feet?'

'No, Nikhil.'

He came and kneelled on the floor beside the bed and reached out to pry my feet from under me.

'And what if I only want to touch your feet and tell you how divine you are?'

I turned my face away. He held my feet stroking them gently.

'You have beautiful feet, Bula. As beautiful as the rest of you. Don't keep them away from me.'

I still looked away, stiffening.

He leaned forward and kissed them, very gently at first. The sensation was troubling, strange and pleasurable. I wanted to jerk my feet away and yet they stayed there delighting in these beautiful stirrings.

As with any physical interaction with Nikhil, within minutes the touch turned electric. His cheek rubbed insistently against my shin: our eyes closed, our breathing heavy. He reached out to me, lightly dropping all the files to the floor.

My mother-in-law knocked on the door a little later.

'Nikhil, come for lunch. The whole house is waiting for you.'

He went across to open the door. I hoped she would not notice his hair still bearing the imprint from minutes back of my fingers wound in them.

'Ranga Ma, there is too much work today. Can Bula have lunch with us in the dining hall so that we can finish soon and get back to work?'

She looked imperious.

'No, Nikhil. You eat with the men. Bou-ma will serve you all and only afterwards eat with the rest of the women of the household. Till then you will have to work alone.'

She turned on her heel and left.

I restored the files to the table and rearranged some of the papers neatly.

Then I turned to Nikhil who was sitting looking at me with a relaxed smile. We held hands like naughty schoolchildren on the stairs and up to the dining hall. He reluctantly let go of my hand then, a gentle touch at the elbow guiding me just half a step before him. I went and took up my place at the sideboard. He sat at the head of the table in the place his father till so recently occupied. He rolled back his kurta sleeves and in his eyes there shone a calm, contented light.

✦

The day had been bitterly cold with howling winds and incessant rain. There was a pall of moisture and steely cold all over. I woke up in the middle of the night needing to use the bathroom though too fuzzy and sleepy to want to. The urge won over and wrapping the edge of my saree closer to me against the chill, I went to the smaller bathroom I used, next to the stairs on the west wing.

I noticed the square of white light from Nikhil's study window on the passage columns. I knew by now that he read real late into the night.

I switched off the bathroom lights and stepped outside. Nikhil was standing there, a hint of anguish in his eyes. Wordlessly, he led me to an unused bedroom in that west wing and bolted the door.

Tonight it was a different Nikhil from the gentle yielding lover I had known so far. His touch was volatile, fiery, passionate. I leaned against the wall for support as his hands kneaded me, almost bruising. The fingers in my hair clenched so tight they hurt as his lips swooped down in a crushing kiss. When he spoke, his breath was ragged.

'Forgive me, Bula, I am behaving like a beast.'

'Shhh, Nikhil.'

I cradled his head on my shoulder, stroking him.

'I knew you had left your room. I...I couldn't stay away.'

My palms spread out on the skin on his back, holding him closer still. He shivered.

There was complete darkness and utter silence in that tiny room for a very long time. Then he sank to the floor, breathing deep. I sat down with him, in the close circle of his arms, propped up by his knee and his chest.

We still couldn't let go of each other, feeling each other wondrously, wanting far more. He buried his face in my hair.

That night in the velvet black depths of the night, I wanted to tell Nikhil so much. I wanted to pour out all those songs in my heart that he had authored. I wanted him to know that the beast in him had called out to its mate in me that I didn't know could exist and whose identity and fruition gave me such a deep sense of peace. Just as each time he looked in my direction, feelings I didn't know even remotely awoke and clamoured for his touch. That every happy experience I had so far, paled in the utter bliss of just sitting there with him, being held like something precious. That each human being finds that one eternal philosophy to live by and for me it was him!

I still don't know why I couldn't say any of this to him.

His face was still in my hair as he spoke. I could feel the nuzzle of his nose on the side of my neck.

'Did I hurt you? Did I scare you?'

I shook my head.

'Bula, forgive me. To all others I am a model of civility.'

Thoughts crowded my mind in response. I couldn't say the words.

'You have taken away my ability to restrain myself around you.'

It was mutual what this subterfuge and its immense pleasures were. I couldn't utter these thoughts either.

'Only with you do I feel secure enough to express myself, to ask for the fulfilment of my basest desires and to beg that you love me back too. And heaven forbid, if some day we have to be apart; always know that I will live only half a life, half dead almost broken in your absence.'

The thought of losing him made me shiver.

'Damn, you must be cold.' He gathered me closer. 'Come, you must get back to sleep.'

'And you?'

He paused before answering.

'For a long time now I am used to staying up most of the night, unable to sleep. Still I must sleep a bit too.'

'Why are you unable to sleep?'

'Some questions don't have easy answers, Bula. You must sleep now. You have too much menial work to manage without sleep and I don't want you unwell.'

The household was in the grips of deep slumber. Still we walked carefully. At my door I turned to him. Even in that dimness he could tell that something was troubling me.

'What happened, Bula?' he asked softly.

'Please tell me why you are unable to sleep.'

He stayed silent for so long that I thought he wasn't going to answer at all.

'Because, Bula, in the still clarity of the night I am made even more aware that you are alone, accessible, just three doors away from me.'

✦ ✦ ✦

15

Bula: 16 years

When Ashu left for higher studies in Kolkata I felt bereft. There was no way we could write to each other. We wrote of our daily struggles and our emotional dependence on the other and saved them until it could be handed over in person. Each meeting also brought chronicles of how time apart was spent. We wanted to catch up, hold each other and read the notes all at once. Propriety gave us very little opportunity to meet in private. That we could meet at all was because all those who knew us in Phuleshwar had vivid memories of how inseparable we were since childhood.

The first year was agony. Each parting was almost a physical pain. When we met in a couple of month's time it was tinged with the sadness that this was a prelude to yet another separation.

As time progressed, each of us took different paths. Ashu began tasting a new life, enjoying independence, growing into manhood and readying himself for a headier future. I began taking refuge in memories, clinging to things of the past and refusing to allow time to flow by with the new in place of the old. On later visits Ashu became a lot quieter, more thoughtful.

On one visit he did not come over to see me all day. Finally I went over the next morning a little after breakfast. His mother and sister were delicate, superior women who thought that Ashu's association with me should by now have been outgrown. They weren't very happy to have me drop in.

Ashu sat at an impressive desk in his bedroom with thick books strewn all across his heavy four-poster bed. He was a lot thinner and wore glasses now. He glanced up at me, his pen still poised on the page he was making notes in.

'How are you?'

'Fine. You?'

We could have been a couple of strangers.

'I'm well, thank you. Are you busy?'

Then he put his pen away and moved to clear a place on the bed.

'Not really. Come sit here.'

'Do you have to study very hard these days? All these books...'

'Yes, the studies are quite advanced. I have to work hard to keep up. There are many boys who come to my college from the top schools in West Bengal. Our government school in Phuleshwar did not give us that great a grounding. Especially in the Sciences.'

I felt that he was putting down Phuleshwar and all in it, including me. With the old Ashu I would have reacted, bristling. Now I felt a little snubbed and tried not to let it show.

'Where are my letters?

'I didn't have time for letters.'

'Didn't have time for me, you mean.'

'Life in a hostel is very different. There is too much for me to cope with.'

'So I am a burden now.'

'I didn't say that.'

'Then what is it that you are saying?'

'Bula, my life is complicated now. It is no longer about being a schoolboy and running all over the place with you.'

'That is all your life in the past has been?'

'Why are we doing this?'

'Ashu, do you realise how it feels? To continue to live here. To see each place rich in memories of you. To wait for you. To dream about you. To have no life anymore, now that you are gone.'

I found tears streaming down my cheeks. He drew me into his arms and held me.

'Bula, I'm sorry. I didn't mean to make you cry.'

He stroked my hair.

'It's not any easier for me. In a way I envy you that everything around you is the same.'

'It's not. Without you, nothing is the same.'

He didn't reply. Just gave me a very sad smile.

✦ ✦ ✦

16

Bula: 27 years

One day, I couldn't fathom why, Nikhil withdrew. He wouldn't look at me or talk to me until compelled by the conversation to.

I thought he needed his space for a bit and let him be for a while. It was excruciatingly lonely. In fact it was far worse than when I hadn't known him at all and was trying to fit into the household as a scared and abused bride. Then I didn't have to contend with this feeling of something integral to me being torn away.

On Sundays when we met, he would remain courteous though aloof and sat very carefully avoiding all physical contact. These times were the worst. Just entering the room and staying behind closed doors with him triggered constant memories of delicious moments of togetherness we had spent here.

I recall reaching out and holding his hand one day. He let it lay in both of mine, inert, like a dead fish. After a polite wait, he drew it away.

'Nikhil, have I said or done something terrible?'

He would avoid looking at me.

'Why would you think that?'

'You won't even look at me!'

He would look at me then meeting my eye briefly before looking at some point beyond my head. I would feel miserable and let the topic go.

The guilt alone was murderous. One day I decided to pursue the matter again. When we finished part of our work, I turned to him.

'Nikhil, please look at me.'

He did.

'May I kiss you? I miss you so much.'

His mouth opened as if to say something but he remained silent.

I leaned forward and very tentatively met his lips with mine. He sat like a stone statue. My lips savoured the feel of his after the long drought. My head moved willing him to respond. It was like kissing a corpse. When he drew back his eyes were closed. And when he looked at me as one would at a stranger, remote as ever. I looked away stricken, my eyes full of tears.

Many months into this phase, I began to counsel myself to accept this new reality. After all he had a beautiful, sophisticated wife and a child now. Why would he continue to pursue an illicit relationship with someone like me?

Yet it was impossible. Every time I saw him, my resolve would break and I would long to be an active part of his life again. In the silence of the nights when things got so painful I could feel my heart broken. I would relive each and every memory of our earlier intimacies. The earnest timbre of his voice, the sweetness of his touch would all be recounted greedily over and over in my mind.

Unable to help myself, I broached the topic again. We had finished work for the day and Nikhil was just putting away things, ready to leave.

'Even a criminal is informed of the crime he is accused of and given a chance to defend himself. Why are you condemning me in silence?'

'There is no crime.'

'Then why are you treating me like a criminal?'

He stayed silent.

'Nikhil, I want to die. I simply cannot go on like this. The other part, I can understand. At least talk to me as before.'

He walked up to a shuttered window and stood there. Suddenly he punched the wall beside it three times, really hard.

'Nikhil!' I shrieked.

I ran to him and held his hand, trembling. I held it up to my eyes and then kissed it many times. He jerked his hand away and left the room.

✦

One evening Nikhil was not at dinner with the others. A close friend of Akhil's from college, called Niranjan Babu had come to Kolkata on a job hunt. He had moved in with us. The two of them and the twins were the only ones at dinner. Aukhoy Babu had gone to an all-night *keertan* at Dakshinpada.

'Where is Nikhil?' I asked Sraboni.

'He is not coming home tonight. He sent word with Chaudhuri Babu that he would go to see the child. After all every man needs to be with his wife sometime,' my mother-in-law answered.

I continued ladling the fish and the vegetables into individual serving bowls.

I couldn't eat much at dinner. I had a mild headache coming on. Instead of reading by the glow of my bedside lamp, I turned to the wall and fell asleep soon. Around midnight I woke up. The headache was all but gone. There was an empty heaviness in its place. The room felt oppressive and I found myself going out to the verandah. I could smell the heady fragrance of some night-blooming flowers, jasmine perhaps. The trees rustled in the breeze and despite the cold, the verandah offered a haven. I sat on my cane chair hugging my knees in the cool embrace of the dark. A movement on the far right corner of the long verandah caught my eye.

Nikhil stood leaning on the balustrade, his chin cupped in his hands. He wore only pyjama bottoms that gleamed ivory in the dim moonlight. We both looked at each other, aware of the other's presence almost simultaneously. I think it was forever that we froze, unable to pull our gaze away. As if suddenly aware that he could walk if he wanted to, Nikhil took slow faltering steps to where I sat.

He stood before me. Even in that darkness I could see his dark tormented eyes. Battered and unsure where I stood with him, I was still swept away in this strange desire to erase the pain. I reached out to hold his face and with my fingers I stroked his eyes. He slowly knelt before me and hid his face against me, holding me tight. All I knew was that I wanted to give him back all the peace and love, the beauty he had brought to my parched life. And as I soothed him with tender strokes, a deeper sense of peace filled me.

We sat like that for a long long time. It had gotten bitterly cold then. I got up and led him to my bed. We lay beside each other nestling in the warmth of our togetherness, holding each other a little awkwardly, loosely. Still holding each other, we fell asleep.

When I woke up at dawn, he was gone. Only a dent on the pillow beside me served as stark proof that it was not all a dream.

✦

As unobtrusive in death as he had been in life, my father-in-law was found dead in bed at lunchtime. The doctor was of the opinion he had died peacefully in his sleep the night before. It felt sad what was mourned more by Aukhoy Babu and his mother was his will that declared all his assets, company shares and property rights were now Nikhil's.

✦ ✦ ✦

17

Bula: 27 years

Reba came back to the mansion almost seventeen months after she had left to go to her parent's place. There was suddenly a lot more noise and activity on our floor. The baby, Tathagata, was a thin weak child, colicky and given to crying late into the night.

I rarely saw Nikhil. Since that night when we had chanced upon each other in the verandah and had slept in each other's arms, he rarely spoke to me. When he did, it was only about work.

Now when I sat down to tea on my chair in the verandah, Reba would sometimes join me as she used to way back in the past. Mostly she would complain about her weakness and how demanding the baby was. But once in a while she would complain about Nikhil too. I found out that for long now he slept alone in his study. Reba was supremely confident about her beauty and its power. She couldn't understand how Nikhil failed to be besotted by her. She complained bitterly that it was the soulless line of work he was in that had robbed him of high taste and finer feeling, and that now he was a crude bore of a man who did not deserve a wife of her quality and breeding.

Work had grown truly demanding. There were now fourteen large godowns to oversee. Besides the company had just turned distributors for a couple of reputed international consumer goods brands and had started extensive network and logistics operations covering all of Kolkata and the 24 Paraganas. Work was hectic and every Sunday I found it harder and harder to keep up.

As we sat in the locked room hard at work through the whole of Sunday mornings, the air between us crackled with an unspoken tension, a sensual energy that refused to die down. I would dream of reaching out, touching him, melting in his arms as before. His unsmiling face and distant demeanour held me back. I hunched down, stifling those unreasonable desires in me. The work consumed us. We tackled immense amounts of work together, grasping its numbing powers greedily as it diverted me from the pain within.

We had been requesting Akhil and Niranjan Babu to help out a little, even promising the latter a good job in the firm. But they never took it up, preferring to sleep in their rooms till midday before dressing and going off to explore the allure of the city lights together. They both grew more sharply dressed, more refined in their manners and inseparable companions.

✦

'*Achchha didi*, you are the only member of the household who spends so much time with him, does he talk to you?' Reba asked me once.

'No, Reba. He doesn't talk to me, just the minimal information pertaining to work.'

'I really don't understand the man! What makes him tick? He hardly even looks at me or answers my questions.'

This conversation was not easy on me.

'He is a good man. Some men are silent and deep.'

'No didi. I think he is just uncultured. I have been married off to the wrong man. My parents did not think of me and my delicate tastes at all when they pushed me into this awful situation. I knew it right from the beginning. Dark ugly man. No graces or refinement. Almost no redeeming qualities even. You hardly go out so you don't know what delicious men there are in Kolkata. I don't want to be stuck to someone this boring.'

'Now that the baby has come along I am sure things will improve and you will all be a happy family together.'

'The baby...he doesn't even come near it.'

✦

Later that week, only Aukhoy Babu and Nikhil were at dinner. I requested Sraboni to sit with the baby and send Reba down. I told her to serve the men while I kept the individual serving bowls ready.

The men were talking about a large donation Aukhoy Babu wanted to make to a temple in Baranagar to be sponsored by the company.

I normally never spoke at all on occasions like this. Nikhil had taken away my option of speaking to him, anyway. I still spoke out. I think it was the realisation that he played such a large role in the nurture of my daughters that I felt I had a duty to his son.

'Reba says you don't spend time with Tathagata. As it is he has come here late. He needs his father too.'

Nikhil kept silent and continued eating. Finally he said:

'I am not comfortable holding something so tiny and delicate. Tell Reba that is what this household has servants for.'

Reba bristled with fury.

'Ask him didi which of the servants can I take to bed to serve as my husband then?'

Nikhil pushed back his plate with a screech and strode out from the room. I ran after him agitated, crestfallen at what I had done.

'Nikhil, don't leave your food and go off. I'm sorry I said what I did. I...I hadn't thought it through.'

As he stepped on the first of the flight of stairs up I clasped his arm to hold him back. He looked down at my hand and then at my face.

'Please don't go. Please finish your dinner. We all know you work too hard these days.'

Tears brimmed in my eyes. He mustered a bitter smile.

'Come, then.'

When we went back to the room, Reba stood with her hands on her hips ready for a fight.

'Stupid idiot! Never walk out when I am in the room. Don't know your manners....'

'Reba, please go back to the baby. He'll just finish his dinner and join you.'

Luckily for me she decided to postpone the fight and went away muttering and stomping.

'I don't like agitations like this at home,' Aukhoy Babu said disapprovingly.

'It's not Bula's fault. She was only trying to help, Kishore-da,' Nikhil replied. 'Let's forget that scene.'

Then addressing me he asked smiling, 'When will you make your banana flower mocha curry? It's very tasty. I like the way you prepare prawns too. Been a while we've had either.'

✦

I don't think Reba ever bothered to come down to the dining room after that. Nikhil also took to coming home very late. And the later he got, the more worried sick I would be about him being caught in a gory accident. After coming home, he would bathe and then come down for dinner. By then it would be too late for the domestic help or for my mother-in-law and invariably I would be the only one around to serve him.

I began to savour these stray stolen moments I got with him. It also served as a good opportunity for me to catch up with the developments in the office so I was more prepared each Sunday and did not need long-winded explanations to many decisions taken. Often he would explain each major business decision in great detail. Slowly, he began speaking more, more freely and animatedly.

Some part of me missed our earlier intimacy; especially when I was by myself each night. Yet slowly I was making peace with what seemed to be my normal life after the major transgression that we both had faltered into due to our youth and immaturity. Would I like these transgressions to be my life? It wasn't my choice. I had to respect Nikhil's.

Then a telegram came informing me that my mother was very ill and that I should go over immediately. I had then been married about six years. My visits to home had been practically non-existent. I did not feel like going back to Phuleshwar anymore. I did go over as often as possible to see my mother when she visited her brother in our locality. These visits were brief and I was very cautious to mask the reality of my life as Aukhoy Babu's wedded wife.

The telegram had been delivered to my mother-in-law, who had then informed me. I asked her for permission to go. She was reluctant and said she needed to talk to Aukhoy Babu in the evening and together they would decide what arrangements were to be made.

Around seven that evening, a second telegram came informing us that my mother had passed away.

I went down to serve Nikhil dinner as usual. I found my mother-in-law and Aukhoy Babu also sitting at the table conferring.

As I entered, Nikhil looked hard at me and registered my red-rimmed eyes.

'Why did you need to come down to serve me today? Ranga Ma could do it.'

'It's alright.'

'No, it's not. Someone should have let you know that you need not come down and they would do it for one day instead. In this place, the people who work have to die working while the others will take up no responsibility.'

Then, turning to the others he said:

'Ranga Ma, enough discussion...I will drive Bula down to Phuleshwar early in the morning. We will stay there a couple of days until the main ceremonies are done and then I will bring her back.'

'Excellent,' Aukhoy Babu said relieved, his non-existent chin bobbing gravely. 'You all know, I have to be in Katwa.'

'How can that be?' my mother-in-law objected sharply. 'You have your own family. There is the business.'

'Bula is my family, too.'

'You have too much work as it is. No, Nikhil, you cannot go.'

'Will Kishore-da take her? Will Akhil or Niru? Will you? So there is no other option except letting her go alone or with a servant. She is a member of our family. Someone close to her had died. Work or no, I will go with her myself.'

+ + +

18

Bula: 18 years

Ashu's visits to Phuleshwar got rarer still. He later told me of his newfound passion for debating and how most weekends he participated in debate competitions at various venues, all over Kolkata. He had also joined the astronomy club at college and how that entailed weekend visits to rural areas where the city lights did not drown out the star shine. Most of the time, he spent studying hard. By the dint of his concentration he had climbed to the position of one of the class toppers in his Physics Honours batch.

I tried to participate in his new life, feeling genuinely happy when he told me of his achievements.

In reality, life had become very tough for me. Ashu had been the anchor of my life. Without him I had no one to really talk to, to see the better side of me and to inspire me to make a better life for myself.

My father had not been in touch for over eight years then. My mother had bottomed out all her reserves, even the reserves of goodwill she had among her relatives and friends. Sometimes I would lie awake hearing my mother crying in the silence of the night. I would begin to panic at what would happen next.

My fervent dream was that Ashu would settle down soon and come back and take me away. I knew no other person I could turn to. And I thought we had a relationship in which he would not be able to bring himself to see me flounder and sink like this. But ever so often a more practical, more worldly-wise side to me would realise with every passing day this beautiful end to all my wretchedness was turning more and more bleak.

✦ ✦ ✦

19

Bula: 27 years

We drove away the next morning in the pale light of dawn, in complete silence. Only Sujoya woke up and served us both our morning tea in our own rooms. She stood at the gate helping with the bags and watched us set off, before closing the gates again.

By now my mind was tired and confused. I sat in the passenger seat, almost in a stupor. Slowly memories of my mother in happier days flitted before my eyes. Growing up at home was such an innocent joyful time till I was nine and my father withdrew. Even after that, there was a trusting goodness in my mother that the hard times had not destroyed. When she saw others better off than her she felt immensely happy for them, genuinely admiring that piece of jewellery or saree, thankful at being given the opportunity to see and appreciate them.

Suddenly I saw her as a woman – something I never thought of before. She must have been barely twenty seven or so, my age now, when my father withdrew from her life. Did she spend her entire life unfulfilled, drawing solace from my existence? Had I ever consciously done anything to alleviate her suffering?

The car came to a stop. That change in the momentum of the car snapped my reverie and I came awake to my surroundings. We were caught at a level crossing among a large convoy of bullock carts all laden with hay. I had been crying, the dampness on my face alerted me.

I began fumbling for a handkerchief in my purse.

'Here.' he gave me his.

I took it gratefully, wiping the tears away.

As we approached Phuleshwar, the recollection of the roads to be taken came back to me with startling clarity. I gave him direction, until the car pulled up at our small wooden gate.

'Are you alright?' he asked me.

Tears welled up in my eyes but I managed a small smile, thankful to have him here with me. Our eyes held for a moment and then I had to take a deep breath and brace myself to the tragedy of this visit.

The house was crowded with lots of relatives, neighbours and friends of my mother, many of whom I did not know. Chaos ruled foremost.

My mother had attended a *Satyanarayan* puja at a neighbour's house. The traditional *prasad* included an offering called *shirni – atta,* fruits and nuts mixed in milk. Something went wrong with the mix. Perhaps some fruit was too acidic and reacted with the milk. Perhaps the mixture sat in the brass container for too long. About twenty-six people were violently sick with food poisoning. Six died: among them, my mother.

My father came for a very short time accompanied by his other wife, a coarse fat woman. He looked unhappy, wanting to get away. Someone suggested that he stay and perform the last rites. After all she had died as a married woman. My father excused himself.

'Yes we were married. But that was a long time ago. Now there is really no relation. Why should I perform ceremonies for someone else?'

I wanted to do it myself. I still regret that I didn't. It would have been my solemn duty had I been a boy. I didn't see how gender mattered.

'No, not you.... It is not easy on a woman. Trust me, I have done a few funerals now,' Nikhil countered my suggestion.

Finally a cousin, Ma's brother's son was chosen for the task.

I was in a daze. Every minute someone swept me away somewhere and told me of things that needed to be done. Often a relative would hold me tight and begin weeping. The fleeting moments that I saw Nikhil in the crowd I could see him take charge. Under his confident organisation much of the chaos dissipated.

It was he who drove to the district hospital and got the body released with the requisite certification. All the preparations for the last rites were laid out by the time the hearse arrived. The priest performed the ceremony solemnly. My mother lay looking as beautiful and innocent as she had been in life. People had dressed her like a bride. My heart felt anew the pain she had suffered all her life, almost thankful that merciful death had spared her further misery.

When the body was taken away, I went outside into the gardens and sat weeping silently by the ponds, now lush and thick with the tall reeds of jute.

As evening fell the group of people who had gone for the cremation returned. They needed to take a bath. Nikhil had been led to the bathroom at the back of the house. A cousin was occupying it. He chose to bathe by the tap outside. I laid out his towel and clothes on a wooden bench a little further away, a part of me a little ashamed to put him through hardship he probably never had encountered in the comforts of his Kolkata residence. After he had dried himself, I took him to my tiny room to rest for a while.

Somebody made tea. I took a cup in for him. He took a deep almost noisy sip. I then realised he had not eaten all day. I felt a deep pang.

'Are you hungry? I don't even know what to give you? Or how?'

'Don't worry. I'm fine. We will eat when all the others eat something. This cup of tea is a rare gift.'

'Doesn't someone give you tea when you come home?'

'Sometimes I am offered some by Haradhon Kaka or Sujoya. I normally refuse.'

'Why?'

He reverted to his normal silence.

'I...I guess you would need your rest now,' I said, shutting the door gently behind me.

I bumped into an unmarried cousin.

'Your husband is very nice,' she simpered.

'Oh, my! That is not her husband,' another cousin said saucily. 'So who is this gorgeous man, Bula?'

'He is Nikhil, my husband's business partner. My husband is away at Katwa. So Nikhil brought me here.'

'You are lucky, aren't you? Your own house and car and a nice big family to be married into...'

As evening fell, everyone assembled into our sitting room. In turns people sang simple bhajans, in effect asking for peace for the soul of the departed and for the minds of those bereaved. It was a touching cathartic ceremony that gave me a sense of peace. Nikhil had also come in and sat quietly at the back, his eyes closed, hands folded on his lap.

✦

The final ceremonies were conducted and the house emptied out by the next evening. Only Nikhil and I were there for the night. A few neighbours came in for the evening prayers. The bhajans sounded solemn and sweet. Someone had brought dinner packed in a carrier. It was arranged that I would return the container and hand over the keys on our way out the next morning.

I had also been told in the course of the day that according to my mother's will the house now belonged to me. I walked around the house aimlessly. Then I pulled myself together knowing that things needed to be done.

I went into my parent's large bedroom. My mother had left it very neat. A few drops of her *sindoor* lay on her dresser top having fallen when she applied it last. I stared at them poignantly aware that though she continued applying the sindoor, the relationship it stood for had disappeared long back leaving her vacant. I lovingly packed away her sindoor, combs and *kajol* into a small drawer below. I drew the crocheted cover across the mirror. A sense of deep sorrow and regret for her life gripped me.

'Would you need some help?' Nikhil asked me from the doorway.

'Nothing else needs to be done,' I told him. 'Let's go eat and then sleep. We will need to start off early tomorrow.'

As I served the food onto plates, he helped me efficiently. He washed the spoons and filled the glasses with water. We spoke a little while we ate. Rather I spoke, to distract myself. I reminisced about my childhood. I recalled simple incidents that exemplified my mother's spirit. After dinner was done, he insisted on clearing the dishes and washing them. I was horrified. I don't think he had ever done that in his life. But he was adamant.

I stood beside the sink while he washed.

'I used to watch you, out beyond the kitchen gardens after our huge Sunday meals. You were dumped with big stacks of dishes. Let me do it just this once.'

He had chosen to sleep on the narrow divan in the hall. I went to my childhood room which seemed miniscule compared to the dimensions of the rooms in the Kolkata house. If I had expected the comfort of the familiar, it wasn't forthcoming. Everything seemed very distant, alien. And sleep wouldn't come easy.

I woke up fairly early almost at dawn. I let myself out for a walk about on the grounds. After drifting around aimlessly, I came back to sit on the wooden bench out at the back. Nikhil came upon me there accidentally, seemed inclined to retreat but stayed. His eyes looked out beyond.

'This place seems like a beautiful place to grow up in. Did you have a happy childhood?'

'Mostly.'

'My childhood was not that great.'

'Why?'

'I don't really know. I don't think our house has the right atmosphere for growing kids. It's too formal. Almost repressive somehow....'

'Don't you have happy memories?'

'A few.... All of them involve being given money or gifts. Guess that's what made me a businessman.'

'No human being ever made you happy?'

'Some did, back then. But as I grew up I realised they were only nice because they expected a big handout from my father in return.'

'Poor little rich boy!'

'I don't think I ever had someone in my life to just talk to.'

'You grew up in a house with four other boys. It can't be true.'

'Kishore-da was always after one impractical pursuit after another. Akhil is like what you see him now, sweet and self-centred. The twins are another age group altogether.'

'What about friends?'

'Flotsam and jetsam.... They drifted in and out.'

'So what did you do back then?'

'Amused myself, mostly. Developed a twisted mind, I think. I always see things differently.'

'I don't think it's true.' I mused. 'It meant a lot to me that you came here with me. I can't imagine how I would have done it alone.'

For a moment I was overwhelmed by the imminence of a sense of loss. Then I blurted out.

'In a way, I am happy for her that she died.'

'Why?'

'It liberated her. Her life was very lonely. She was broken-hearted.'

'You think death is preferable to living without a man?'

'Not any man. That one man!'

'That's awful! How can you say that?'

✦ ✦ ✦

20

Bula: 20 years

Ashu did not come home immediately after his exam ended in early May. The heat and the humidity only made my wait for him even more excruciating. All around the mango and jamun trees hung heavy with ripe fruits. Everything I saw seemed fulfilled and made a mockery of my own hollowness.

That evening, my mother had gone to spend a weekend with an old aunt in Kharagpur. Left to myself I decided to combat both the heat and the gnawing restlessness within me by taking a walk along the Ganga.

There was a thin path beside the road along the embankment, meant for pedestrians to keep out of the way of the vehicles. I walked along it slowly, lost in a world of my own.

'Bula!' I heard a familiar voice call out.

It was Ashu. He seemed to be going somewhere special with his sister. Both were dressed incredibly smart and a little out of place for Phuleshwar. I became acutely aware of my crumpled cotton saree and the sun-faded blouse.

I mustered a smile.

'So nice to see you here unexpectedly, Bula!'

'Do you know Dada is going abroad for his studies?' his sister burst out excitedly.

'Hold it, Madhobi,' he admonished her. 'I wanted to tell her myself.... Yes, I've been accepted for the Masters in Astrophysics course at Case Western University. One other student from my college has made it. She will be studying Philosophy.'

I stared at him with unseeing eyes. That old feeling of a heavy band wound around my chest and didn't let me breathe.

'Are you alright?'

I stared at him bewildered. How could I be alright? How could he ask me that?

'I...uh...I am fine. Congratulations!'

I think Madhobi chattered on excitedly for a couple of minutes after that and I tried to respond the best I could, my eyes fixed on the swirling grey waters below us.

Finally, they drove off with a cheery wave of the hand. I couldn't move. I stood transfixed.

I didn't know when the Ganga grew dark and brooding. Or when the menacing monsoon clouds gathered overhead. When I came to my senses I felt the tingling lashes of the season's first rains hurting my skin.

✦ ✦ ✦

21

Bula: 27 years

We had barely driven for half an hour when we encountered a thunderstorm. Everything around us grew a belligerent grey with menacing winds tossing things in the air.

'Bula, I can't see a thing. We need to stop for a while.'

Nikhil found a place under a huge banyan tree that stood towering beside what seemed like a canal. We sat in silence watching the dust swirling in the raging winds.

As I looked through the windows unclear, disjointed, unhappy thoughts swirled about in me. The two days here with Nikhil around had been so beautiful. Especially the few conversations we'd had. Once we went back to the Krishnapur household, would I lose him again? Like my father had been lost? I thought of my poor mother. What was it in us that the men we loved found it so easy to walk away? Poor Ma, a lifetime of what I had been through this past year and then simply dying one day. Was the same in store for me?

'I know you are about to cry. I can read it in your face.'

What would he know how it felt to mourn the passing of my mother. With her gone, I was now truly alone in this hostile wide world. The wind roared furiously. Now small stones hit the windshield and the sides of the car. I began to speak more to distract myself, my voice small.

'I was a little older than eleven when it happened. My father had deserted my mother. He had not come home, not even in the evening for a cup of tea or something like that for over a year by then. My mother wept all the time or lay in bed, sick. The family life, all the security I knew was just tossed around like that leaf you see in the wind.

Then one day just as I was leaving school, my father stood a little away from the school gates with his bicycle. I felt so happy to see him. I had known all along he loved me too much. I knew he would come back for me. I shouted out to him as I'd rushed to meet him. As I reached him he looked at me puzzled as if I were a stranger. I told him I was glad he had come back and now we could go home together. He looked first bewildered and then a little embarrassed. A fat kid with fair skin and frizzled brown hair, about my age, walked up to him and held his hand and turning to me asked him, "Who is she, Baba?" He did not reply. He held her hand tight and quickly led her away.'

I had stood and watched him go, feeling as if my life were draining out of me. So long it had been my bitterest memory of loss. Now there were others. As acrid, as inexplicable.

'I have been thinking...'

I needed a gulp of air to go on. Outside the storm gathered even more threateningly. I braved it.

'Now with Ma gone, there really is no other reason to go back, you know. I had signed the papers, I had negotiated all of it only for Ma. The girls could go to school here. In time, I could find something to do too.'

Now that I really could do all of this, it felt as repugnant as it had felt alluring all these years. A fresh rush of wind almost shook the car and made me cower a little.

'And you, Bula? Is that what you really want?'

I had to look at him. And as my eyes met his I shook my head very slow. Almost unbidden, so much spilled over.

'Come to me, Bula.'

As I turned to him, unsure I'd heard right, he reached out and gathered me to him. He stroked my hair, murmuring, as I turned my face to his chest. With her gone, I was now truly alone in this hostile wide world.

The wind howled outside. He held me tenderly as I wept like a dam had burst inside me. My tears poured all over his punjabi front. His hands held me lightly. Suddenly I was aware that he was crying too, softly, only the small shudders of irregular breath giving him away.

'Nikhil, what's wrong? Now look what I've done.'

I took the *anchol* of my saree and carefully wiped away his tears, devastated at his sorrow. Finally he spoke.

'Bula, what a nasty, unholy mess we are in!'

I held him close.

'No, Nikhil. What a wonderful peaceful haven we have built to shield ourselves from the nasty, unholy, indecent world outside. This is the only antidote to my life.'

'How tough was this past year for you, Bula? I want to know.'

I couldn't answer. He gathered roughly me to his chest then, his stubble grazing my forehead.

'Forgive me. This is neither the time nor the place... Bula, staying away from you was, is and will be the toughest thing I ever have to do. With you gone, every happiness and sustenance is gone too.'

'I couldn't tell. You looked so remote, so in control...'

'When we sat together every Sunday, I just longed to touch you just once. I longed to lay my face against the hollow of your neck and breathe in your fragrance.'

'Why didn't you?'

'It's a long story, Bula.' His voice was dry and low. He ran a weary hand through his hair. 'I have been a witness to the treatment meted out to you. Anybody in your situation would gladly turn towards respite. By coming into your life, providing companionship and requesting for attention frequently, I created a feeling of trust. I betrayed that trust, Bula. Both yours and Kishore-da's. I had my own agenda. I loved you. And that love made me so blind that I had to have you no matter what.

'I exploited the situation. At that time I thought I was giving you support. But in reality my being there was threatening your world. You are entitled to a happy marriage, Bula. Kishore-da is a little obsessed with godliness and generally weak in nature. But he is a good man, someone I have grown up with. I realised that you are too good to refuse anyone anything. And what I was asking for was earth-shattering – infidelity! And each time I asked, you came to me no matter what the cost to your own happiness.'

I listened in silence unable to comprehend what he was saying.

'At one point my love matured. I wanted to be the one to give more than I got. I wanted to give you a chance at happiness.

Sacrificing my happiness for yours hasn't been easy. But it is the most important thing for me now.'

'Is this why you have avoided me all these months?'

'I'm sorry if I hurt you. I only wanted your greater happiness.'

'Hurt? Happiness? I had no reason to go on living, Nikhil – except my duty to my two little daughters. Seeing their faces stopped me. That and the fleeting bittersweet moments I managed to find with you.'

'That is the scenario I have created, Bula. If I hadn't, you would have reconciled to life with Kishore-da and you would have found ways to be happy with him.'

I freed myself to sit up then. He looked concerned, putting an arm around my shoulders, concerned.

'To you, I am a victim of circumstances who would sleep with the first man who spoke nicely to her, am I?'

'That's not what I meant.'

'So I would sleep with Chaudhuri Kaku, Haradhon, Akhil, Niru Babu, Mukunda, Durlabh, the sweeper, the carpenter – any man who was nice to me before you, and would have me?'

'Bula!'

I felt so angry with him: angry at the dumb assumptions he had made and furious that he had put me through all this agony on such baseless wild imaginings. But just as swiftly as the rage had seized me, it subsided into a sense of intense sorrow.

My fingers played with his hair.

'You are so wise and yet so dense, Nikhil. You cannot see your own beauty. I did not come to you as an escape. I was drawn to you on the strength of who you are.'

'How do you know who I am? I had, and always will have, an ulterior motive, an indecent one.'

I leaned sideways and kissed him. Not gently as in the past, but deeply, urgently, informing him of the fires within. My touch was no longer a gentle reminder of love, but a demonstration that I yearned for his body and had missed it far too long. The kiss was intoxicating and left us both breathless. When we surfaced I asked him:

'How indecent did that feel?'

He shook his head, trying not to drown as we both had.

'Would you like to know why? Because when you and I reach out to each other it is to someone we trust the most, our best friend, our soul mate and the love of our life.'

'Bula, I can give you nothing in return. I have nothing left to give you.'

'Do you love me, Nikhil?'

His voice grew husky.

'Do you still need to be told?'

'Then there is nothing more you can give me.'

'I've been thinking, Bula, all of last night. These past few months you have been like a zombie. I haven't seen you smile once. You have dark circles under your eyes. You look unhappy and unwell. And now, though your mother has died, you look healthier, wholesome and happier than you have done in a long time. I cannot believe it, but I begin to wonder. Does having me near you make so much of a difference to your well-being?'

To me it was a rhetorical question.

'Answer me, Bula. It is important.'

I couldn't find an answer in words. Instead the hand that went up to his right shoulder just gripped him firmer.

'Bula, you know I have put myself through hell all this time to try and save your marriage. It didn't occur to me throughout that maybe there is nothing in your marriage to save...that it may be just as hollow and unsustainable as mine.

'I like to have evidence to back my hypothesis and I've sat up all night trying to recall one incident, one sign from all these six years that Kishore-da cares for you. And do you know what? I can't think of one word or one gesture, not a single glance or action. Then I tell myself that I have grown up with him, I know him better than you or most other people in the world. Would I give my Bula away to him for safekeeping?

'The answer is pure and simple. I can't!'

He drew me in even tighter and, bending, lay his cheek against mine. We let the fierce dust storm outside play out its passion, shield ours. He slowly drew out my chain and unclasping it, freed the diamond ring.

The wind stilled a little. Small raindrops bespattered the glass now.

'You wanted to befriend the rain, didn't you? Let's ask your friend to be an eternal witness to my promise.'

The heavens parted and enormous raindrops cascaded happily all around us. He slipped the ring on.

'I promise to always love and cherish you. I promise you friendship, laughter and loyalty for the rest of0 my life. And above all, I promise I will never hurt you or leave you as I have so misguidedly done recently. Now kiss me, Bula! For this is our marriage. The only marriage that could ever matter.'

✦ ✦ ✦

22

Bula: 27 years

We got back in time for a late lunch. Reba had taken the baby and left for her parents place. She had left a message.

'Tell him to come and beg me to come back if he wants me around.'

My mother-in-law conveyed it to him with flashing eyes.

'Please don't give me your opinions on this matter, Ranga Ma,' Nikhil told her.

She still went off on a long tirade about family responsibilities and how she was perplexed by his strangely misplaced sense of duty towards me in all matters.

'I don't want to argue with you. I am not going to give you any explanation. And I'm not going to sit here and listen to this nonsense.'

He left the table; his plate barely touched and went to wash up at the back of the room.

My mother-in-law went off into an agitation.

'I am the closest you have to a mother. If you go off-track, I need to bring you back. Only I can tell you what's best for you.'

I stood amidst it all, a mute, miserable spectator. My mother-in-law then turned to me in fury and I shrank from what she was going to say next. She spotted my ring.

'Who has made you wear a diamond ring now?'

I looked down. That simple ceremony and the magic of the drive back had made me forget to string it back hidden away on my chain.

'It...it was my mother's. She left me this. And her house.'

'She had such huge diamond? Why didn't she give you decent ornaments for the wedding then?'

'Maybe this was special to her and she wanted me to have it only now.'

I slipped away from the room as soon as I could after clearing away the table. I went and sat on my cane chair in the verandah, still a little shaky. In a while Nikhil came out and seeing me walked up. His face looked a little troubled.

'I'm sorry about the scene back there.'

'Don't be. I am well aware I'm the root cause.'

'Did you get to eat anything?'

'No, I didn't feel like.'

'Let's get the car to go and eat out somewhere.'

'You're crazy! The world will truly come to an end, if we did.'

'Doesn't it bother you, how we always make compromises with life? Never really doing,what we most wish to.'

'Try your best to accept it.'

'Why do we have to?'

'To buy peace, I guess. To avoid having scenes like this all the time.'

'I was planning to go down to the office a little later. Would you come down to the drawing room. Help me finish some of our work here itself.'

His eyes looked fatigued. I could see how the hectic events of the past few days would have drained him out completely.

'You go down and begin. I'll be there in a few minutes.'

Then I did something unprecedented in my time in the household. I went out to the servant's outhouse. An undermaid, Maya, was sitting vacantly on a culvert. Together we woke up Sujoya. I gave them the necessary instructions.

Then I went to the smaller drawing room. Nikhil was already deep in some papers. He raised his head as he heard me come in.

'Come, sit here.'

✦

Dinner that night was a full house. Apart from all the males in the house, there were two visiting relatives, Bireshwar Babu and his son Biswajeet.

My mother-in-law was supervising the meal, in an obviously foul mood. Even the seasoned Haradhon Kaku was jumpy. I stood way back in the background, almost regretting having come.

'I heard, Bou-ma that the kitchen fires were relit this afternoon,' she fired at me almost through gritted teeth.

My head bowed. It was an act of avoidance.

'Have you forgotten who you are, your place in this household? Nobody knows better than you your position right from the day you came into this house. You are no better than a servant here. How dare you presume to disrupt our routine?

'Really, Sulochona Debi, you must not upset Ma,' Aukhoy Babu bleated.

'He did not have lunch. In Phuleshwar as well, we could not light our fires and so we only ate what neighbours gave us.'

'Look at her answer me like this. Kishore, your wife is overreaching her limits.'

'I was tired and very hungry and Bula arranged food for me, Ranga Ma. Why does that upset you?' Nikhil spoke up. 'Why is it that every time I sit down to eat, you have to start something?'

'You are also forgetting your place Nikhil.'

'No, I am sorry Ranga Ma, you are forgetting your responsibilities.

'Look at all these people in this room. See them carefully, all of them. Only two here are actually working hard day and night to keep this household running. All the rest have an easy ride. So do you want to know who the two are? Bula. And me.

'And now you tell me she can't get food cooked in her own kitchen. And that I have no right to food here? Where did you get that idea?'

He looked around the full table of gawking faces.

'And since everybody is here, let me also talk about a matter that is important. You should all know how things are.

'Bankim Kaku was Baba's partner. Our company is a partnership company. You all know that when Bankim Kaku died he left all his shares and claims in the business to me. Baba willed everything he owned to me too, which means for a while I was the sole owner. It is a tough responsibility. For very long now I have tried my best to get Kishore-da involved. He hasn't been. Legally and otherwise as well, I have greater comfort if I have a partner. As you all know, for over three years now Bula has been working hard alongside me. Last year, I decided formally to make her a partner in the firm. The company that feeds and runs this house belongs in part to her. In the eyes of the law, this house also belongs to the company, which means in a roundabout way there are actually only two owners of this house – Bula and me.'

Gasps from around the table greeted this announcement. I hadn't known this. I looked at Nikhil stunned. He had turned to face his spluttering Ranga Ma.

'You cannot do this. My husband shamed and cheated us all by willing everything he had to you. But that you will go and put it all on the name of this...this two-bit whore you fancy, it cannot be tolerated. We all know what kind of woman she is. No respect for my son. No graces to keep him with her. And her slow seduction of you, knowing that you are wealthy. I have had enough of this immoral association. You cannot be allowed to get away with this.'

Food was forgotten by everyone.

'Ranga Ma, I will not tolerate this language in the house! I have heard you speak horribly to Bula all along and I did not interfere thinking she is your family. But family means respect, and love. And that I see nothing of. Simply because we are all tolerant of you doesn't mean you can get as insulting as you like.'

'You are giving me a lecture? I have been like your mother, been your mother after she died. I have brought you up.'

'You will always have the respect that is due to you.'

'You call this respect? Neither I nor any member of my family will stay here even for one more night. Come Kishore!'

'Where will we go, Ma?' Aukhoy Babu asked almost dazed by the turn of events.

'We will sleep on the streets and beg for our food, but I will not stay here to be insulted.'

'You can both go, if you like. If consideration for me doesn't stop you, my words most certainly won't. But Bula will stay here and so will all the kids.'

He turned to the twins.

'You want to stay here, don't you?'

They both nodded.

'Bula. Bula. Bula. From the day you called her that instead of Bou-di I knew something was wrong! We should all go and she should stay here with you. As what? Your queen? Aren't you ashamed to have this unnatural attraction for Kishore's wife?

He looked at her and replied calmly.

'You can say what you want, Ranga Ma. You can call it an unnatural attraction. Or seduction. Or whatever other filth you choose. You can get as disgusting as you want to be. It doesn't bother me. It doesn't change a thing.'

'And what will your wife have to say about it, huh?'

'I think all those in this household whose lifestyles are sponsored by our hard work had better not have anything to say.'

'You mean us. That we eat and live on what you provide. Nikhil, I didn't grow old slaving for this household to hear this today. I am leaving immediately. Come Kishore. And you,' she almost spat out her anger in my direction.

'Bula will not go. And in I've had enough of this nonsense. Sraboni, take Ranga Ma to her room,' he rapped out loud.

For a moment it seemed she had more in her arsenal. I think it was the open talk about money and ownership that defeated her. That taken away seemed to have robbed her of most of her power too. Perhaps because all her life that is what she recognised.

He turned back to the group on the table. Something about the way he sat and held his shoulders reminded us of the quiet power his father had wielded. It demanded respect.

'I'm sorry about that. Now that all the unpleasantness is out of the way, let's eat.'

'Nikhil, you can't do this,' Aukhoy Babu weakly began. 'The shares: I don't want them in my wife's name. Transfer them to me right away.'

'Why? Bored of your bhajan-keertan? And wife? Whose wife? When was Bula ever your wife? I have never seen you behave like a husband even once. The fact is Kishore-da, I do not have to have a partner. I chose to have one, preferably from my family. I had to take a very painful decision. Among all in this household, who is the most reliable? Who would take care of the others, no matter what, even if I were not around? I have seen the care you have taken of Bula and your brothers or even your kids all these years. And by uncomplainingly putting up with all your nonsense she has proved that she is the more stable one. Besides she wanted to learn the work and has done an excellent job so far. She has great potential. I don't need a partner who wants the money. I need a partner who can generate the money, someone who wishes to work at it and is capable of doing it, too. In all ways, Bula is what I need.'

He patiently though firmly ended Aukhoy Babu's further feeble protests.

Then I saw Nikhil in his elements, a rare event. He began to speak lightly about hilarious incidents in his office and managed to create as light and easy atmosphere in the dining room as feasible under the circumstances. I soaked up half-heard the anecdotes coming forward to help Haradhon Kaku if a plate or bowl fell empty.

The next morning, my mother-in-law left for a visit to her family home in Belghoria where her four brothers lived.

In the space of an evening, an era had come to an end.

Nikhil waited as I collected the dishes for the maids to carry downstairs. My mind was in a whirl. The fury of my mother-in-law's words stood out the most. He gauged my thoughts.

'I didn't know even after so long that if you scratch the surface you would find a common fish wife. Though now I am glad she has said those things. However crudely put.'

My movements slowed a little, winded. It had been a stormy day in more ways than could be recounted. I'd turned to organise the leftovers. It felt odd that he hung around.

'Aren't you going to sleep?'

He paused before answering.

'I'm hoping my presence would spare you further unpleasantness for tonight.'

'And are you planning to stand guard over me all my life? Or just for tonight?'

I'd asked half-joking but I saw his expression harden and realised it was a tasteless tactless thing to say. But he did wait for me and we went up to the top floor we occupied together. In a way, he was right. My mother-in-law's rants served to free me from that burden of secrecy. Once enunciated so crudely,

I no longer cared what it could seem like to the rest of the household. We spoke as went up the stairs.

'Why did you make me your business partner? When?'

'Very long ago. To make sure you never go away from me. Ever!'

'Then why would you want to avoid me all these months?'

'I was willing to give you a chance at your happiness, not absolute freedom, not escape from me. I still wanted to be around to care for and protect you, no matter what.'

'Too bad, that's what I was planning on doing with you,' I joked.

At my room, he came in too. He never had this late in the night before. I did not remark upon it either. We both knew the rules of the game had changed imperceptibly. He stopped just inside the doorway and looked around the room.

'Do you recall I used to play with the girls here and in the next room when it was their nursery?'

'Yes, Nikhil.' I paused. 'I remember every moment you have spent with me.'

'That was my family, the greatest warmth I had ever known in my life. Each night I found it more difficult to leave. I just wanted to beg you to let me be a part of your life and keep me here with you.'

'As far back as that?'

He nodded. Now he came to sit at the edge of the bed.

'Do you know when I first fell in love with you? You were serving us all your first rice as a bride. You were like a scared deer. I knew there was immense pain inside you. I could sense you were exhausted. And yet you followed the contradictory orders of a horde of pernickety older women of the family with great dignity. To me the rice you served was ambrosia. Yet I was miserable. Of all the women in the world I did not want to be in love with this young girl married into my household. I kept telling myself what I felt was just the strangeness of having someone new around.

'I used to hear Ranga Ma abuse you. She is foolish and indiscreet. I wondered at Kishore-da's blindness. Why couldn't he stand up for you – scared, innocent, delicate and lovely? After all, you were his bride. I was too afraid to...afraid that people would then know my true feelings for you.

I waited to see you at meal times. If you went past me on the staircase I would feel my breath constrict. The pain of loving you made me grow up much faster. Sometimes I feel so weighed down by this terrible truth, so weary.

'When Ranga Ma insisted that I marry Reba, I should have refused. I should have remained unattached, free. In my misery I thought marriage would reform me. It was a mistake. Perhaps I am incapable of loving another. Perhaps it is Reba as a person. I never had a married life. I never had the warmth and happiness I get by simply sitting here with you.'

I stared at him. I had never known. Back then I was incapable of even dreaming this up.

'I stole every minute I possibly could with you. Every night after the household feel asleep, I wanted to come and sit on your bed and ask you whether you missed me as badly as I did in the lonely depths of the night. It got so bad that I made myself take an oath that I would never set foot in this room unless specifically asked to by the kids or you.'

'And what if I specifically ask you now to never leave this room?'

'Then I never will!'

Nikhil didn't leave that night. Neither have we spent a night apart since, except when he had to travel. My palms felt him wonderingly, unable to believe that Nikhil was really back and was really holding me.

'It's been far too long,' he groaned. 'Let's promise that whatever happens we won't do this to ourselves.'

'I had no choice in the matter. It was your bizarre decision all the way.'

'And yet you kissed me and still loved me through it all. You amaze me, Bula. Why would you put up with somebody like me?'

'I thought you had begun to love Reba and were reaffirming your vows to her. I tried so hard to let you go. Oh, Nikhil!'

All through the night we spoke to each other of our pain and our longings. Sometimes words were not needed. We made love unhurriedly and thoroughly, completely comfortable in the custody of the other.

'Would you find it difficult to trust me now?'

'I trust you. I trusted you even when you did not want to speak to me. Whatever happens, Nikhil, don't stop speaking to me. I can survive without Nikhil the lover, but without Nikhil the friend I will surely die.'

'But Nikhil the friend is your lover, how can you distinguish between them? Accept me as I am, Bula, flaws, idiosyncrasies and all. Accept that I sometimes don't simply want your words alone, but all of you as well.'

'I have never withheld myself, Nikhil. I have always given you whatever I can of myself.'

I demonstrated that.

'Did it hurt when I didn't return your kisses?'

'Intolerably. Almost as badly as when you smashed your hand on the wall.'

We smiled at the recollection.

'Bula, I have been very stupid, haven't I?'

'To think that you consider Aukhoy Babu important enough to forego this. Yeah, extremely stupid!'

'I can sense he has hurt you so badly, that I am amazed you can trust a man again.'

I moved away and sat on the chair, troubled by the memories his statement recalled. Then haltingly I found myself telling Nikhil of the few times the hypocritical and devout Aukhoy Babu thrust himself on me.

'Believe me Nikhil after he was done with me, I would be terrified if I ever saw a man twenty feet away. I don't know how you made a place for yourself in my life. With you I feel so secure. I feel I have found a safe haven at last.'

'One part of me wishes I could go down to his room and break a few bones. I'll choose to look at the brighter side, though. You wouldn't even have looked at me, but for this behaviour on his part.'

'No, Nikhil, I love you so much, I may even have left a good man for you. Thank God he has given me a guiltless choice.'

✦ ✦ ✦

23

Bula: 27 years

One night as we lay exhausted, his fingers absently stroking me, he asked me.

'What should I do about Reba?'

'Nikhil, what can I say?'

'Help me out, *na*.'

'I really haven't given it any thought.'

'Somehow, I have begun this quest of relentlessly simplifying my life. Cutting Reba off completely would be ideal. Should I do that?'

'If I had gone away, would you have advised Aukhoy Babu to come and get me?'

'It's a different case, Bula. Besides you never left him and went away. Not after all you had to go through. If you went away, I would not waste my time trying to advise anybody. I would have come and pleaded with you to come back to my life. Would you have come back?'

'I have a theory, Nikhil.'

His fingers in my hair created sensation that almost made me forget.

'There really are no villains. There is simply compatibility or not. Believe me, we must have hurt and pained Aukhoy Babu and Reba as deeply as they have us too. Two different belief systems. Two different continents. And in the midst of all of this, isn't it just a miracle that there's me and you?'

He turned and kissed me long and hard then.

'I don't even want to think, even theoretically, of a time when you aren't here. And conversely, have you noticed how lovely and peaceful everything is now without Ranga Ma and Reba?'

'Still, Nikhil, this is their home.'

'You know what I really want right now? I want to go back with you to Phuleshwar. I want to live with you, just the two of us. I want to sit in your gardens among the many little ponds. Take me away with you, Bula, to your house. Keep me with you.'

'I can't Nikhil. There are the little girls. There is Tathagata. In the eyes of others, Aukhoy Babu and Reba matter as well. True we owe nobody anything. And so we will do exactly as we please. But here. Without making things obvious.'

'And that is the question I am asking you. What should I do about Reba? Doesn't it make more sense to divorce her and be free for life?'

'Assume you divorce Reba and I divorce, you know, him; what real difference would it make in our lives?'

'We could marry instead of technically committing a "sin" each time we are together.'

Suddenly we were on the verge of another occurring again. I still kept the conversation going.

'Does the technicality bother you that much?'

'I thought it would bother you that you do not bear my name and social sanction.'

'No, it doesn't.'

'Think it through, Bula.'

Though technically we were both floating past sentient thought. I fought to be lucid.

'No really, Nikhil. The way our lives are placed there are too many other players involved. Would the household continue undisturbed? You are responsible for my mother-in-law and the twins. Even if you made a settlement on them it would not be the same. They would have to give up their rhythm of life and start afresh. Our kids would possibly be looked upon with contempt outside. The divorces are really not worth it. All that matters to me is that you love me and you will be by my side. For me your word matters a lot more than any legality. We have both seen the institution of marriage very closely. I don't know about you, but it holds no further charm for me.'

'Do you know something, Bula? I don't think any businessman I know would have made such a clear and well thought out presentation defending a decision. I'm so proud of you!'

'Thanks!' I nibbled him. 'And, Nikhil?'

"Hmmm?"

'I am done talking....'

And the night moved on to wordless eloquence.

✦

One morning later that week, Nikhil picked up Ma and together they went to pick up Reba.

I almost couldn't recognise Reba. She had cut her hair short and wore it heavily lacquered in a weird poufy style. Her face was thin and unsmiling, heavily powdered and with vivid black eye make-up. She no longer wore the hand-woven sarees we did. Instead she wore heavily-sequined transparent synthetic ones with low neck-lined and sleeveless blouses. She had chosen to leave behind Tathagata.

My mother-in-law looked exactly the same she had done these past few years, except that she seemed to have aged about ten years in these two months that she had been away. Instead of that irascible haughty personality, there was an older more vulnerable air about her.

I had been privy to the fact that her brother's wives had all resented her demands and interference in their lives over the years. On festivals and special occasions when they visited, they would tell me horror stories about her curbs on them and tell me to be very careful. Now I concluded her visit there had finally proven to be too much for them and they may have not been as accommodating as she would have liked.

An appropriate lunch had been prepared and I served them both.

'How is Tito? Why didn't you bring him? I requested you there so many times,' my mother-in-law started.

'I really have no time for that child. I have left him there with the servants who take care of him. Besides from now on I want to go out for a lot of parties and functions and I don't want him to get in the way.'

'Some more fish, Reba?'

'No, didi. I am eating less. I have to get slim and maintain my figure.'

'Bou-ma, can I have her piece of fish?' My mother-in-law asked tentatively.

'Yes, of course.' I quickly served a couple of fish slices in a bowl and left it beside her plate.

Actually widows are not permitted non-vegetarian fare in our families. To me it always seemed a cruel practice. How can someone be expected to completely give up a life time's dietary habit one fine day? If someone did not mourn the death of a husband, would a food restriction compel them to?

For the first time I saw my mother-in-law in a humane light. Of course there will always be the generation gap. While she was giving me hell, she was only acting out of what the narrow confines of her life had taught her. In her own way, she was protecting her turf. Her resentment of me probably coincided with the awareness that she was growing old and being edged out by those who came after.

'Tha'mma, you should not eat fish!' Deetu spoke up.

'Deetu, don't talk rubbish,' I scolded her.

'Why didi? Why should Tha'mma not eat fish?' Geetu piped up.

'Okay, you two. Finish your food fast and go.'

Once they were gone, my mother-in-law asked a little cowed.

'The kids...they won't tell anyone, will they?'

'Ma, what you choose to eat in your own home is nobody else's concern,' I reassured her.

From the next evening onwards, the whole household would hear Reba engaged in an increasingly hysterical high-pitched conversation with Nikhil. When he came down for dinner, he still looked calm and impassive and went back to his study as he did in the past. To sleep however, he came to our room. In bed at night, he refused to talk about it to me at all. I wasn't really interested. But was concerned about the unpleasantness Nikhil had to face on a nightly basis.

At dinner time once, my mother-in-law spoke up.

'Nikhil, what does Reba want? Why is there an argument every night?'

'Nothing, Ranga Ma.'

'How can it be nothing? Every evening all of us hear her.'

He looked around the table. Everyone had stopped eating.

'She wants to go out every night to parties and all. I have given her my blessings and offered her the car. But she wants me to go along.'

'So take her. She is modern girl from the city. Not somebody who will just sit at home like your Bou-di.'

'But I need somebody like Bula. After a full day of work, I just want to come home to a smiling face and a peaceful evening, eat my dinner and read my books.'

'You work too hard, Nikhil. But you have to please your wife too.'

'That wife I don't think I can please. And really I have no desire to.'

He looked at me.

'Bula advised me to get Reba back. So I did. Beyond that I am afraid I will do no more.'

After a particularly vicious rant at night, Reba would leave for her parent's home the next morning. She would return in a few weeks of her own accord. This became a fixed pattern.

+ + +

24

Bula: 19 years

Ashu came by the next day. I chose to speak to him near the small little pond in our garden. We were quite close to my favourite little pond which once yielded blue lotuses. Today it was a putrid mess of dried and rotting water hyacinth. A little way off there stood an ancient wooden bench battered by countless vagaries of the weather.

We sat on this bench, Ashu plainly uncomfortable and I, numb and deadened.

He placed a palm on my folded hands.

'Aren't you happy for me? I had hoped that as my friend you would rejoice at this stupendous opportunity I have been given.'

I couldn't answer. I could only look down at his hand. His fingers were creamy white in colour against which the vivid black hairs stood out, the bones fine and long. His fingers were neatly manicured. I stared at them mesmerised at their beauty, their familiarity raising a lump in my throat.

'Why aren't you speaking to me, Bula?'

'I don't have much to say, Ashutosh Babu.'

'Come on, Bula. I don't want to go away like this. I want my last memories of you to be beautiful, memorable, a testament to our childhood. Give me one last kiss. Give me something unforgettable to sustain me through all those cold nights abroad.'

I turned my palm upward and entwined my fingers in his.

✦ ✦ ✦

25

Bula: 28 years

My mother-in-law began refusing food. I was a little worried that she was depressed or irritable in the face of the recent upheavals in her life. It turned out to be jaundice. She lay in her room, listless.

Nikhil had a large colour television installed in her bedroom so that she had the choice of entertainment through her illness. I went down to her room at meal times and tried my best to coax her to eat the unpalatable diet prescribed.

It was during one such dinner that Nikhil came into the room, just back from work.

'Bula, I need some tea. Please could you put some ginger in it,' he asked as he sat down on a chair letting out a deep breath. 'How are you today Ranga Ma?'

'Pulling along as usual. And this make me tea-coffee, you should be telling your wife, Nikhil, not your Bou-di '

I had just set her water down and was about to leave. Nikhil let out a mirthless laugh.

'Ranga Ma, then I will never get tea in all my life. No its better to ask for what I want where I know I will get it.'

'I am worried about you and Reba.'

He continued as if he hadn't heard her say that.

'And do you know the beauty of it? Kishore-da never wants to have tea. So if Bula ever wants to make tea, it can only be for me.'

For a moment it seemed to me as if everybody in the room was well aware that it was not tea that was being spoken of at all. I left the room hurriedly.

I came back with his cup of tea and the salted biscuits he liked on a tray. I handed him his cup and went back to bring my mother-in-law's boiled papaya dinner.

Nikhil looked at me with a lazy smile and then went back to talking.

'But nothing has really changed Ranga Ma. Okay tell me, don't I still touch your feet every morning and spend time with you before I leave home? When I come back, don't I first see your face and then go for my bath? Where do you see the change? Has Bula been rude to you? After the efforts she has been putting into the business and now that she is a partner of the firm, she is a fairly rich woman. And she still makes me my tea every evening and feeds you your dinner.

'If you start thinking all kinds of things, you will only make yourself ill.'

He took a long sip of the tea.

'Great tea, Bula. Thanks!'

Then turning to her, he said softly. His expression very earnest, making it clear these were matters he had given deep thought to.

'What Bankim Kaku did not do, I could have done in five minutes, Ranga Ma. I could have given those shares to Kishore-da, or money equivalent to it. I don't mean to be disrespectful, but I am afraid he will go and donate it all to some temple or spend it all on his hanger-on friends. Bankim Kaku thought of you and the twins when he did what he did. Your place is in this house. Your life here will remain unchanged.

'And, you are needlessly wary about Bula being a partner. I trust her as much a more worried sick I would be about s I do because of the person she is. I trust her with my life. In fact, in my will she gets everything. I know she will do the right thing for the whole family. Don't worry, Ranga Ma, you are in good hands.

'Nothing has changed. Nothing will!'

✦

Asking Reba for tea was just a figment of my mother-in-law's imagination. Though she had moved back with an outrageous array of suitcases, she was never in this house, often coming in around lunchtime and leaving after tea. Somehow, both Aukhoy Babu and she were never seriously considered to be family members anymore.

The phone in my bedroom rang. Normally it would be a call from the office for some clarifications or Nikhil affording himself the briefest respite from the tedium of his day. He would say:

'Had lunch?'

'Not yet.'

'It's late. Go eat something.'

'Have you eaten?'

'Just finished. Thought I'd speak to you before getting back to work.'

'Feels nice to hear your voice.'

'Ditto. What delayed your going down for lunch?'

'You won't approve if I told you.'

'Tell me anyway.'

'I was reading *Rebecca*.'

'I wish you would outgrow your passion for romance.'

'Really?'

'Let me rephrase that: the passion for reading second grade romance novels.'

I would be amused. I would say.

'You know, I think you would make a terrific romance novelist.'

'Pray why?'

'Because of who you are.'

'You see a side to me no one else does. Maybe that side doesn't exist at all. And maybe it's all your imagination....'

'Didn't I say wonderful romance writer?'

'You got me,' he'd say. 'I love you.'

'Ditto.'

'Can't you give a man slogging in a stuffy office a little happiness? Say the words.'

'You have to earn them.'

'Can I buy them instead?'

'How much would you pay?'

'You know I can only pay in kind.'

'Okay. What would you pay?'

His voice would grow solemn.

'Everlasting love. Till death do us part...'

I wouldn't be able to answer. I knew he meant every word. He was that kind of man.

'I love you. With all my heart!'

He'd laugh, happy. I listen marvelling at how much light and hope had flooded into my life serendipitously.

'Now go and have lunch.'

'See you tonight.'

'If you promise to sit with me and work on some of these figures, I will come home early.

'Of course. What figures? The Jagadeeshpur godown? Yeah that needs a lot of work.'

'Let me wind up as soon as I can and then I'll leave. Okay?'

This time however it was Reba. Her voice sounded different, younger slightly fake and breathless.

'Didi, it's me, Reba.'

'Hello, Reba. How are you?'

'Great! You won't believe what I am doing right now. Can you guess?'

'No, Reba.'

'I knew nobody would be able to guess. I'm acting in a movie! Can you believe it? I'm a movie star! The producer has totally flipped over my looks. Keeps saying I have such a fresh face and figure he can't believe I'm married. I haven't told anybody about Tathagata. Why give away your age? In this business it matters a lot.

'So anyway, shooting in the studios begins day after tomorrow. I am not the lead heroine. I am the bad lady. I would ideally like to have got the heroine's part. But the banner is so big I wanted to make my debut with them whatever it took.

Then there are location shoots in Chandipore and Kalimpong. I'm very excited.'

'Congrats!'

'There is one favour I wanted to ask of you, though. I have to tell Nikhil about this. You know how bad-tempered and scary he is. I can't approach him. The only person he listens to is you. Will you please tell him?'

'Reba, don't misunderstand me. I think you owe it to him to tell him directly.'

'Please didi. You tell him first. I will call later and talk about it.'

✦

That evening, Nikhil was home in time for dinner and it was one of those occasions when dinner prolonged into a large *adda* with everyone's fingers drying, caked with food. Without thinking it through I did what hadn't ever before. I blurted out:

'Nikhil, I need to speak to you. Alone.'

My mother-in-law glared at me.

'What could you have to say to Nikhil that we cannot hear?'

'It's...it's about Reba.'

'What about Reba? Tell us all. We would all like to know.'

I stood silent, unsure what to do next.

'Ranga Ma, stop cross-questioning her. She must have her reasons. Come, Bula.'

And Nikhil ushered me out into the passage outside.

'What is it, Bula?'

I hesitated as I spoke.

'I had a call from her. This afternoon. She wanted me to prepare you before she speaks to you herself. She has been offered a part in a film and has taken it up.'

'Okay,' he said his face impassive. 'Shall we go back inside?'

He went back to his meal unfazed. But Ranga Ma wouldn't hold her peace prodding him until he announced to the whole crowd of curious faces.

'Reba has just become a heroine in the Bangla film industry.'

Pandemonium broke out at this announcement, mainly fuelled by my mother-in-law.

'Actress? In our family? Our name will be mud! Nikhil, you must stop her.'

Aukhoy Babu warmly agreed with his mother. Akhil wondered aloud whether this meant complimentary film tickets for life. He and Niru Babu began to discuss all the delicious possibilities.

My mother-in-law turned to me frowning and furious.

'Bou-ma, you should have come to me with this immediately. I would have called her father and by the time I had finished, this acting fever would have been cold.'

'It's my issue we are talking about. Bula did the right thing by coming to me first.'

'If she goes ahead with this Nikhil, just divorce her. I will find you a better bride, more beautiful and stable, not one to go running off to her father's place the instant the lime slips off the *paan* leaf. Poor boy, almost never had a married life.'

My mother-in-law commiserated, completely forgetting that she was the one who had hand-picked Reba in the first place.

'Why are you all making a big deal of it? Reba wants to be an actress, let her be one. Just the other day Bula and I were talking about the pros and cons of divorcing her. Bula was against the idea and now I see her wisdom. This acting thing means I'm completely free of her. I don't even need to go to the lawyers anymore.'

'But what will our friends, our society say about us?' my mother-in-law practically wailed.

'Our family had its full share of all kinds of freaks and freeloaders. Reba's choice of vocation is just another one. Let her act. Let her be happy, too.'

A few months later, one of the film magazines Reba had subscribed to had been delivered and it stood on a table on the outer verandah. The cover bore a startling picture of Reba in a revealing heavily sequined costume, with unnatural slits all over. Her face was bloated, with heavy pancake make-up and a plastic smile. Nikhil looked at it absently. Then recognising her likeness shook his head a little and slid it under a pile of similar magazines.

✦ ✦ ✦

26

Bula: 29 years

The kids were playing noisily on the verandah. I was trying to curb them.

'Nikhil will be reading or working. Don't make a noise and disturb him. Go down and play in the courtyard.'

He heard me. He came out of his study with a smile.

'Hey!' he greeted all of us. 'Let them be. Sometimes it's a boon to be dragged away from Nietzsche.'

He grabbed Geetu's pigtail.

'Why aren't you talking to me?'

'Ma said you are working and should not be disturbed.'

'But I got disturbed anyway, *na*?'

'Then let's go down and play cricket.'

'Geetu madam, your school is shut on Saturdays, but poor Nikhil still has to go to work.'

'Don't go for one day. Or work with Ma in the small drawing room.'

'Excellent idea!'

Deetu came up to him and pointed to a gap in her mouth.

'I lost this tooth yesterday, Nikhil.'

'My, you look all grown up.'

'No I look weird. My teeth look gappy.'

'The new tooth that will come will be very beautiful. And you will then have a beautiful smile, like your Ma.'

'Really?'

All three bantered some more. Then Nikhil straightened and looked at me.

'What are you doing today?'

'Nothing. The usual.'

'I was thinking, let's all go for a weekend to Digha. Ranga Ma has also been unwell. The sea air will also do her good. We will all get a brief break.'

'You should persuade her.' Then I added. 'Nikhil, I wanted to ask you something.'

'Hmmm?'

'I am okay with English now, the reading part. I mean, at least I am better than before. But I still need the confidence to speak fluently. There is a lady, Mrs. Beck, who can come and give me lessons. I would have them on three weekday afternoons.

'Good. Start them.'

I swallowed.

'About her payment...I have no money.'

'What do you mean you have no money?'

I felt miserable. I looked down.

'Your allowance won't cover it then? How much will her fees be? For how many months does she need to be paid now? Let me know and by tomorrow I will have the money ready.'

I looked at him bewildered still stuck on his first question.

'My allowance...?'

He stared at me.

'Doesn't Kishore-da give you money every month?'

I shook my head.

'What? Bula, at the beginning of every month Chaudhuri Kaku comes down to the house to give each member of this family including the twins, an allowance from the company profits. Kishore-da has been getting four thousand a month since the day you were married and since the kids came along it is eight thousand rupees and, of which it is explicit that four thousand is to be handed over to you. Ranga Ma's money used to be given to Bankim Kaku. Chaudhuri Kaku just followed that convention and I never thought to tell him otherwise.'

'I have never had any money, Nikhil.'

'How do you buy your sarees or other personal essentials then?'

I looked at him not certain I should have started this conversation at all.

'I wear what I get as Sashti and puja gifts from relatives. And I have been careful with what I got at the time of my marriage.'

'Clothes? You have never gone shopping? He has never bought you some?'

I shook my head. He looked thunderous.

'Why didn't you tell me that you wear clothes that other people give you? And that since you came to this household you have had no money and never gone shopping?'

I nodded, unhappily.

'Damn! Who gets you your soap, shampoo, oil and all the things women need?'

'I manage with what I can get from the kitchen.'

He leaned against a wall and rested the back of his head too, his chin pointing up. When he spoke I could sense intense anger.

'And you never thought I needed to know this?'

'I didn't know...' I began in a small voice.

How would I know how large business families functioned?

'Does he buy the girls what they need, their clothes?'

I thought it prudent not to answer. He stood like that looking up, unseeing, at the sky. Finally he spoke.

'It was stupid of me not to have seen it. Knowing the man, I should have anticipated it. Even after all this I unthinkingly didn't expect him to stoop so low, considering him worthy of at least this bit of trust. It's my dumb fault.'

'It's okay,' I tried reassuring him.

'No, it's not okay,' he exploded. 'How low can a man get? And how much of this nonsense will you keep putting up with? I simply can't understand why you do these really stupid things?'

He walked over to the verandah railing and looked into the garden below.

✦

He came in almost at seven. There was a major traffic snarl. I was in the kitchen and Sujoya came to call me. He was coming out of my mother-in-law's room.

'Hi!'

'Do you feel like some tea?'

'Tea would be great. Especially when I didn't have time for lunch today. Can you bring it to my study?'

I had made him some cheese sandwiches too, which were his favourite. It hurt to be told that he had skipped lunch. As I handed him his cup of tea, he held out a large envelope.

'What is it?'

'It's a form for your personal bank account. You need to sign it where it is marked with a red 'X'. I'll take care of the rest.'

I sat on his bed and opening the envelope tugged at the papers inside. There was a sheaf of forms pinned together and as they pulled free, a pile of paper money fell on to the bed. I stared at it.

'What's the money for?'

'That's your spending money for now.'

I seemed like an awful lot. As if reading my mind, he said, 'It's ten thousand.'

'That's a lot of money,' I said, suddenly thinking of my mother and how she would keep small notes of one and two rupees tied to the end of her saree.

He brought his cup of tea and sat beside me on the bed. His voice was far away.

'It was the end of the second year of my graduation with Honours in Economics from St. Xavier's College. I was just twenty years old, Bula. All my professors were encouraging me to apply for a scholarship abroad. Some said Cambridge. Others said Harvard. The Principal, Father Eric, had very kindly been mentoring me and had written glowing recommendations. Those matter more than marks, for admission abroad.

'Then one day, Baba took me to our oldest rice godown, the one in the Sealdah area. There he began explaining the business. He got nostalgic and started telling me about how he began the business on nothing but his wits alone as a refugee from Dhaka in 1948, just to fend for his family. Then he held my hand and told me that if I went away, the business that he had built up grain by grain would probably not survive. Both he and Bankim Babu were aware that Kishore-da had refused to grow responsible or smart about money. The others were all too young.

'I had a bright future ahead of me, Bula. If the fates were good I could have shone on the world stage as an economist. I just looked at all these people. This household needs huge amounts of money to keep running. If the business collapsed, where would they go? Who would take care of them all? As a professor, I may have been able to provide only for Akhil, what about the others? I may not be related to the Chakrabortys but they are my family too. At twenty, I grew up in the space of one day. And for the past eleven years Bula, I have done nothing except try and make the most money I can for this household.

'I don't watch movies. I don't smoke. I only spend on my books and petrol. All my friends from school, college and business host and attend parties. I get invited to some of them too. I don't go. I come straight home, eat whatever is given to me and read my books.

'How little do I matter to you that you couldn't come to me asking for one small thing that you needed?

'Since long, I have been asking you to help with the accounts. You were calculating in lakhs and even crores for me, Bula, when you didn't have two rupees to buy a bar of soap. Our godowns are filled with hundreds of cartons. You know that. You sign off on the inventory lists as often as I do. And yet, you never asked me to get you one.

How do you think it makes me feel?'

✦ ✦ ✦

27

Bula: 29 years

My mother-in-law welcomed the chance to go for a break to Digha. Aukhoy Babu did not want to come, citing a prior appointment. The twins had their examinations and were promised a big treat afterwards. Akhil and Niru Babu, always ready to have fun, were all game.

Finally it was decided that we would all go and take the girls, along with Sraboni to share the responsibilities of looking after them and my mother-in-law's needs. The twins would need a car to ferry them to and from the exam halls. With only one car and six adults and two children to accommodate, the travel details were turning out to be a nightmare. Just then Akhil came up with the idea of borrowing a close friend's Yezdi and the plans were on track again.

We set off early on a Friday morning. Akhil and Niru Babu met us dressed nattily in leather jackets and helmets. Nikhil helped my mother-in-law to her seat at the back with Sraboni and the kids. From the glove compartment Nikhil fished out two enormous orange flavoured lollipops.

'Here, these are for you,' he told the wide-eyed girls. 'And if you want to throw up or go the bathroom, tell me and I will stop, okay?'

'Okay Nikhil,' they replied, still mesmerised by the lollipops.

'Why give them sweets first thing in the morning?' my mother-in-law grumbled.

We wove through the sparser early morning traffic and were soon out of the city limits. At the side of the highway Akhil and Niru stood holding their helmets, looking impatient. Nikhil drew up alongside.

'Must you drive like a tortoise, Dada? We have been waiting here for so long.'

'Akhil, I am not racing you.'

'Race. Race. We want race,' the kids chanted.

Akhil grinned at them.

'Drive safely,' Nikhil shouted as the two bikers zoomed off.

They would slow down deliberately and then speed to catch up again. The kids were all wide-eyed admiration at their antics.

'Ranga Ma, shall we stop for tea?'

'Will there be a nice place? Clean, I mean.'

'You won't get the comforts and the hygiene of home on the road,' he replied grinning.

The tea stall we stopped at was fairly clean as tea stalls go. There were metal tables and fairly new plastic chairs scattered around a small hut. Akhil and Niru joined us, fluffing the hair flattened by their helmets.

'Is this place okay?' Niru asked.

'Whatever Dada – Bou-di like...' Akhil answered.

'Do you want Double Sevens?' Nikhil asked the kids.

They both smiled happily. Looking around at the shack my mother-in-law also hurriedly decided against anything prepared in it.

'A cola for me too, Nikhil.'

'The rest of us are having tea I guess,' Nikhil said and turned to place the order with a shirtless, gap-toothed boy of about ten.

There were a couple of concrete benches and the kids decided to race over and explore their multicoloured delights. Sraboni went over to keep an eye on them.

We were all sipping tea, when Nikhil spoke up, very normally.

'Ranga Ma, I just found out that Kishore-da has never given Bula any of her money. In seven years it works out to be more than three and a half lakhs, without interest. Apart from food, she has been given nothing in the household. Not the basics. Not even a saree. Weren't you aware of it?'

'Each man will have his own ideas of how to provide for his family, Nikhil,' she replied after a while.

'In this case it seems he simply decided not to provide for his family at all,' he said bitterly.

Akhil chipped in. He always had an observation to offer.

'Bou-di does not have a single saree that costs above a hundred rupees. The kids wear terrible, cheap clothes.'

'You knew? Why didn't you tell me?' Nikhil turned to him.

'How was I to know that you are such an ass you wouldn't notice? And why should what people wear be important?'

Nikhil turned slowly to my mother-in-law and looked her straight in the eye.

His voice sank lower. 'To think that Bula has lived with us for close to seven years in utter deprivation and want.... You cannot begin to imagine how deeply this fact pains me.'

My mother-in-law opened her mouth as if to speak and then closed it again. I guess she wanted to protest about the inappropriateness of me being important enough to Nikhil to matter but she thought the better of it. He had said it with such simple earnestness that she had no option but to hear it without demur. Such was the quiet power of Nikhil.

'We are a fairly comfortably-off family, Ranga Ma. There is no way even a servant of the house can be kept in near bondage. Even they are given generous pay packages and very good treatment. What is the use of all my hard work and all the money it brings in, if it does not ease the lives of the people I care about?'

My tone was low. 'Let it go, Nikhil.'

'Talking of money, Dada, I simply love this Yezdi. Can I get one?' Akhil chipped in.

'Absolutely not!'

'So all that money is not easing my life either.'

'Shut up, Akhil. Your life has too much ease as it is. Find some constructive work.'

'I'm too young. Life is too short.'

'Yes, life is too short. And I have had first-hand experience of your riding style today. These two factors mean no bike for you, ever. '

Akhil pouted.

'However, if you like I can get you a car. Paritosh Babu, a business acquaintance, has a Fiat dealership. One condition though – after this you will never ride a bike again.'

He reached out and lightly hit Akhil on the top of his head. 'After all, you are my only liability now.'

'If only Reba had not done what she has and brought us all disgrace...' my mother-in-law mourned.

Nikhil was pulling out his wallet to pay. He dug among the notes absently, looking for the right ones.

'Yeah it is from scary memories like that that we need to run away and take a break.'

The sun had risen a little higher. All on the back seat were dozing off. The roads we needed to take were deserted, except for stray cattle or a straggling villager. Nikhil chose a cassette and inserted it, adjusting the volume way down low. Heartbreakingly beautiful love songs played out one after the other.

As we drew closer to the coast we saw the devastation caused by a recent cyclone. Adobe huts stood bareheaded with the thatch blown away. Palm leaf lean-to shelters lay collapsed. The roads were littered with fallen branches and even a few electric poles. Dark brown puddles glistened among the fields.

We came upon a town called Contai and encountered heavier traffic. Nikhil came to a stop behind a line of heavily laden lorries.

'Why are we stopping? Have we reached?' my mother-in-law spoke up.

My first reaction on hearing her voice was to draw my hand away. Nikhil gripped it firmer, his thumb stroking me to calmness. I still didn't know whether the height of the Ambassador seat hid our entwined fingers from her view.

'No, Ranga Ma. We have come into a town called Contai. There's some traffic here.'

'You get very good *Martaman* bananas here. Buy some, Nikhil.'

'Are you hungry?'

'No, we all had breakfast. The bananas are really good.'

He still drew up next to a line of stalls and got all of us tender coconuts to drink from. He then got off and returned with two enormous bunches of those bananas.

The hotel he had us booked into stood a little away from the main beach, further up, beyond the casuarina woods. There were three large double rooms on the second floor with ample windows that gave us and uninterrupted view of the sand and the waves and the sea birds circling over. Each room had a large double bed and a single bed. And thankfully for my mother-in-law, the attached bathrooms were dry and spotless.

There was a large dining room on this floor where we sat down to lunch after our baths. Akhil decided to order for us all and was getting more and more confused as the choices came in and got complex. He thrust the menu card into Nikhil's hand and said, 'Here Dada, you do it.'

He gave it right back saying, 'You are doing fine. Just slow down a bit, look at each person and hear out their complete order carefully. Then you will remember it all.'

While Akhil stumbled through the order, he added, 'Just remember, Ranga Ma eats only pure vegetarian food.'

'Actually Sudhindro Doctor Babu has recommended that she eat fish, for her arthritis. He says she needs the fish oil in her diet,' I lied.

'Oh. Sorry, Ranga Ma I did not know.'

All through lunch the kids pleaded to go down to the beach. However I wanted them to rest a little. We decided to take a short nap and go down only at four.

I was lying in bed next to the kids reading 'The Agony and the Ecstasy' that I had picked up from among Nikhil's bookshelves in the downstairs passage. There was a knock on the door. It was Nikhil.

'All fine? Do you like your room?'

I nodded. He held out a bulky shopping bag.

'You know how hectic this last week has been. I just managed to get these for the girls.'

The bag contained smart swimsuits, beach towels and bright plastic beach sets.

'Oh, Nikhil! These are all so pretty. The girls will be ecstatic.'

'I'm glad you like them. I had asked Lynette from the office to get all of this for me. I hope the swimwear fits.'

'The material stretches, so I think it will be fine, Thanks.'

He put the stuff away and sat down on the single bed, his back against the wall, legs stretched out over the width of the bed.

'I have asked room service for tea and they will be bringing it soon.'

The tray was delivered almost immediately. I poured the tea, spooned the sugar in and handed him his cup.

'Do you remember telling me about a million fantastic girls in the city of Kolkata...?'

I nodded.

'Out of them all, only you bring me tea, Bula. And to me this is not a cup of tea. It is a reminder that I matter so much to someone that every day she takes time out to make me something I like and bring it to me.'

'But Nikhil, tea is made and given across millions of home. It's nothing out of the ordinary.'

'I love your fascination for demographics and what millions are up to. But that is not the point, Bula.'

✦

Dinner was a subdued affair as the stint at the beach had tired out the kids and my mother-in-law. We returned to our rooms a little before nine. After putting the kids to sleep, I prepared for bed and lay down to resume the reading of my book.

There was a knock on my door. It was Akhil.

'Come chat with us, Bou-di. Why are you sleeping off at nine like old folks?'

I didn't know what to say. I was unsure what was expected of me.

'The kids are sleeping. I can't leave them alone.'

'You'll be in the next room. You are not abandoning them. And given how tired they were they'll sleep soundly all night.'

He almost dragged me by the wrist all the way to the room next door that the three men were sharing. Nikhil and Niru were arguing over who would get the single bed.

'He's your brother, you sleep with him.'

'See Bou-di, all evening these two have been fighting over who will not sleep with me. Like I have rabies or something,' Akhil complained.

Till I left the room late into the night, this argument would resume at frequent intervals.

'He snores and flails about.'

'Your brother, still.'

'No. I do not. This is slander.'

A pack of cards was brought out. I had been brought up to believe that playing cards was a low unladylike activity.

I barely knew how to tell the suits apart. Nikhil and Akhil together explained the intricacies of a game called 28. I tried my best to grasp it. Nikhil chose to partner me as Akhil refused to, appalled I was so raw at playing cards.

'You do not waste your trump suit on a pointless hand.' Nikhil would review my game. 'You need to retain your trump for maximum advantage.'

Or: 'If you have too many cards of one suit, you ought to discard the ones with the most points when your partner is taking that hand.'

I tried to follow the best I could. Nikhil played brilliantly. Akhil was almost as good, except that he made ridiculous bids fuelled by ego and not sense. And Niru played almost as bad as me.

Initially I felt awful each time a blunder on my part made us lose. But over time I learned to relax and get into the spirit of the game. At one point Nikhil suggested we check on the kids together.

'Don't deal till we are back. I don't trust either of you.'

We left the room, holding hands in the corridor. In their sleep the kids huddled together sweetly, holding each other. I tucked the blanket around them.

'I am happy we could have this holiday.'

When we went back to the room, Akhil wanted a ten minute break. He and Niru needed to stretch their legs.

'Let Niru smoke. Don't you use this opportunity to start, Akhil.'

'Dada! Where do you get these weird ideas from?'

'I know you too well. Have fun.'

Akhil did most of the dealing. After each game, Nikhil would coach me. When that was not needed he would just sit back. Sometimes I caught his eyes on me, profound and intent. I noticed with a sense of wonder that they no longer felt vacant anymore. Instead there was this soft glow of tranquillity.

It was after one thirty in the morning that we decided to call it a day. Nikhil wanted to escort me back to my room.

'Niru, when I am back if I find you on the single bed I will bodily pick you up and drop you on Akhil. I promise,' he threatened.

He came into my room with me.

'Did you enjoy the game?'

'I like the game. But I need to play it better to enjoy it.'

'Don't worry. Akhil and I have had plenty of practice. You will catch up.'

He sat on the single bed. He tilted his head first to one side and then the other as if his neck felt sore.

'Bula, please massage my shoulders. I'm stiff from all that driving.'

'They are waiting for you.'

'They are adults. They will understand.'

It was the world's most hopeless massage. Every place my fingers detected stiffness in, I would lean forward and kiss. My hands would intermittently stop kneading and start wandering and caressing. Until I simply gave up and we lay wrapped together so late into the night that it almost didn't make sense for him to go back to the other room anymore.

✦

The beach at Digha was completely wet with sand packed so solid that lorries drove over them with ease. It was a vast sandy strip that met a gentle sea. Much of the beach had large colonies of tiny red crabs that build little sand igloos until the next wave washed them away. I had never been to the sea before and its compelling beauty held me spellbound. Even my mother-in-law seemed cheerful, enjoying this break from her routine life.

Nikhil pulled off his panjabi and carefully kept it where we sat. He folded his jeans up to his knees and grabbing each girl by a hand began to stroll down to the sea. Akhil and Niru followed him bare-bodied too, in shorts.

After a while the girls seemed to have had their fill of the waves and Nikhil brought them to another spot nearer us and started teaching them to build sand castles. All their efforts were pathetic but they had lots of fun messing in the sand with their grubby little fingers. Nikhil came up to me.

'Come for a walk, Bula.'

I hesitated.

'Go. How long will you keep sitting here? Sraboni and I will keep an eye on the kids,' my mother-in-law prompted.

As we set off, Nikhil turned to me.

'Bula, even if I forget, remind me that we need to take a break every three months.'

'Hmmm.'

'Did you have a good time?'

'Yes, very,' I looked up at him with a smile. 'Pity we need to go back after lunch.'

He drew in his breath.

'You look so beautiful. I wish I could kiss you here right now with the sands, the sea, the winds and the sun as my witness.'

'Your Ranga Ma will be your prime witness and will have a heart attack.'

'You think? Want to test your assumption?'

'No! Nikhil!'

'You are a cruel woman, Bula.'

I laughed then.

'Completely. A laughing assassin.'

'I love to hear you laugh. Earlier you seldom did.'

'Earlier I had no reason to.'

'And what reason do you have now?'

We stopped walking and turned towards each other, our eyes hungry. We resumed walking.

'Thank you for getting the girls all that stuff. I think that is the most thoughtful thing anybody has done for them all their lives.'

'You know I don't believe in buying things, especially for kids. However, till you pick up the shopping habit, someone has to get them the basics.'

'If it were not for you Nikhil, they would not know what it means to have a father figure.'

'I am their father, Bula. They are a part of me as much as you are. Only, I don't have a certificate that says so.'

His voice sounded so agonised that I could gauge.

'We'll find a solution to that too, Nikhil. Soon, I promise.'

And as he looked mildly puzzled, I elaborated.

'I know how deeply you grieve the loss of Tathagata and the guilt you grapple with each day for not doing your best for him.'

'I cannot ever express how much I miss my son. And on occasions like this when all of us are together carefree and happy, it gets unbearable.'

'I know. In fact when I advised you against seeking a divorce, Tathagata was a big factor. This way at least you get to see him however rarely, however briefly. In a messy divorce you very well could have lost that privilege altogether.'

'I could try and have him come back, you know Bula, but I don't want to further uproot a child from even the uncertainties of his life with Reba for that is all the security he knows. Thankfully Reba's mother is a wall, a source of such deep strength that I know he is well looked after.'

'We will get him to come to stay, Nikhil. I know we will find a way.'

Though his eyes were hauntingly sad he mustered a knowing smile.

'Though we must take pledge. When he comes, neither of us is allowed to overcompensate and spoil the child.'

I turned away to retort.

'You are the one who spoils the children. In these matters I am always very balanced.'

His steps slowed down and it may have been from the effort to not laugh outright at my assertion.

The breeze blew something in my eye then. I winced and rubbed my eye gently. The eye continued burning.

'Let me see,' he held me lightly by the cheeks and looked in.

'Yeah, there's a black speck. Could be a tiny bug or something.... Hold on for a minute.'

He drew the edge of my saree and expertly though gently held it to my eye. The cloth picked up the speck and the burning sensation ceased. Then he did something that I had only seen my mother do and it left an aching lump in my heart.

He folded the soft material of my saree into a thick pad and breathed on it hard a few times to give it heat and then held it to my eye for fomentation.

'Are you alright?'

'With you by my side, Nikhil, more than ever...'

The girls wanted to go back into the water and he took them obligingly. My mother-in-law wanted a stroll as well and Sraboni went with her. I sat on the boulders at the edge of the sand watching the man I love splash about in the eddies with our children. Akhil and Niru were out in the sea swimming. Then Akhil came out and walked towards me.

'I saw you sitting alone.'

He picked up a towel from the pile and wrapped it around his shoulders. He sat down on the boulder beside me leaving a trail of water flowing down the sides.

We both watched Nikhil in silence.

'He has gone through a lot in his life.'

I didn't pretend I didn't know who he was talking about.

'He is too dutiful and serious: a textbook example of a good man. I wonder where he finds the moral strength to always remain calm and always do the right thing.'

'Yes, he is exceptional.'

'It is only in the past five or six years that I have seen him like this, happy. He feels alive and deeply contented. With all that was happening in his life I wondered how.'

Then Akhil put a lazy arm around me and leaned his wet head on my left shoulder.

'Thank you, Bou-di.'

I didn't ask him what for. He knew he didn't need to elaborate.

My mother-in-law walked up.

'All wet and messy! Now why do you need to hug her?' she grumbled.

Akhil smiled up at her impishly.

'Because she is my Bou-di.'

✦ ✦ ✦

28

Bula: 29 years

Back then in the middle of being administered to by Aukhoy Babu and practically passing out from the unpleasantness of it all, I sometimes used to dream of when he would be out of my life for good or better still dream of something bad happening to him. It felt like justice. It felt like some deep, almost unforgivable, violation would be avenged.

When that actually came to pass however, I had to grapple with a whole lot of unknown emotions the uppermost being pity and perhaps even fear for him and his well-being. It had patently been borne out that he was unlikely to ever learn to fend for himself. However, I had to concede to Nikhil's point of view too. His increasingly erratic behaviour and the simple learning that he could get away with anything that he did was beginning to strain our resources. Soon it would begin to harm others, even the girls.

None of us could have predicted such an end to our enjoyable stint at Digha. The car was lively with all of us relaxed and bronzed. It was approaching dusk when we reached

Krishnapur. As we drew up to the lanes leading to our gates we could hear a strange cacophony of noises – the blaring of a tape of badly-sung devotional music, someone sermonising over a microphone and unrelated chants. As we pulled up to the gates, the sight that greeted us was bizarre.

Huge tents had been put up on the lawns. At one side, large pots of food stood where they had been cooked on open fires leaving large singed patches in the grass. In one of the tents, a stage had been put up, on which sat a large group of strangely garbed men who were ranting into the microphone or bursting into tuneless song in turns.

There were a huge flock of 'holy' men wearing some sort of a sectarian uniform. The bushes in the garden were all festooned with scarlet loincloths, presumably the prescribed underwear for the sect, all hung out to dry. As far as the eye could see there were dried leaf plates and terracotta water tumblers, testimony to a couple of days of feasting.

'What is happening, Nikhil?'

My mother-in-law asked bewildered. Nikhil just stared, dumbstruck. I don't think he had a clue.

'Aukhoy Babu seems to have decided to have a party in our absence, Ma,' I told her.

'What party? How could he....' She began for the first time in her life looking nonplussed.

The kids stared at the strange sight with wide eyes. Akhil and Niru rode in beside us and came to a halt with a screech. Akhil caught sight of the chaos and said, 'Whoa!'

As we walked in through the gates, Aukhoy Babu came up and started speaking to Nikhil all bluff and hearty.

'Come, come, Nikhil. It's a very special occasion for me.'

Five men in strange purple and gold robes came and stood by him. I knew we were surrounded by the inner circle of some esoteric cult.

'This is my new Guru-ji and my *guru-bhais*. Today is the happy occasion of my *deeksha*. Guru-ji this is my mother.'

'I hope the deeksha means that you will leave home and go live in the ashram or wherever. Because Kishore-da after the stunt you have just pulled, there is no way I will allow you to live in this house again.'

'What do you mean, Nikhil? I...I will live here as always. I will meet Guru-ji when needed. Sometimes he will come here as my guest.'

'Wait a minute,' Guru-ji said. 'Isn't this house yours, Aukhoy Babu? That is what we were given to understand. You even promised that in time this mansion could be a branch for our sect.'

'Yes I live here. But...' He looked shiftily from his Guru to Nikhil.

'Our ashram always welcomes everybody. But if you are rich and have property, why live with us? There are more needy souls.'

'Kishore-da, get out,' Nikhil said through clenched teeth. 'And take this whole circus with you.'

'No Nikhil, don't be hasty,' my mother-in-law implored. 'Where will he go?'

'He has nearly three lakhs of Bula's money. That should cushion him for now.'

'Forgive him this time. I will speak to him. This is his home. This life is all he knows. You cannot do this. It's not legal.'

Nikhil looked her straight in the eye.

'I'm sorry Ranga Ma. I have to protect the others, you and myself from this growing madness. And legally too, I can.'

He turned on his heel and walked indoors. The kids clung to me. Though they called him Baba, to them the word probably meant loony old distant relative and no more. He had rarely if ever acknowledged their presence.

'Come let's go inside,' I told them and hastily followed Nikhil.

Even the inside of the house looked like a whirlwind had gone through. It was evident that people had slept and eaten everywhere. Items of furniture were moved from their places and thrown about. Small knick-knacks like vases, ashtrays and bowls had been taken from their various places on the shelves and tables and discarded all over.

'What happened here, Ma?' Geetu asked in a scared voice. She had never seen such a disarray before.

'I think there was a big puja of some sort while we were away.'

'But you said party.'

'Did I? Well I'm not sure puja or party.'

'Then why was Nikhil so angry?'

'I don't know, baby. He must have his reasons.'

I settled the kids in their room. I was in the kitchen boiling the water to make tea. I knew Nikhil needed that.

'Bula!'

I heard Nikhil call from the passage upstairs, outside his room, overlooking the courtyard. This was most unusual. He had never shouted out my name like this before. I stepped into the courtyard and looked up at him.

'Yes. Nikhil?'

'Please ask someone to unload all the bags from the car. I need to go out.'

'Okay. Tea?'

'There's no time.'

I did as asked, identified the different bags and instructed Mukundo to take them to the right rooms. Then I hurried inside hoping to speak to Nikhil. He was coming down the stairs in haste.

'Come with me,' he said tersely.

As we left the house, we saw my mother-in-law sitting on the steps outside looking disconsolate. He stopped beside her.

'Ranga Ma, there is some emergency in Chaudhuri Kaka's family. I have to go. I'm taking Bula with me.'

Then he stopped by the knot of chairs on which the sect leaders were sitting.

'I'm sorry. We are not inhospitable people. It is only that I wish we all had been informed about his event. This has been a most inopportune time. I would appreciate it if you could wrap up now and leave.'

'Even we have been misled, son. We would not have come like this. Aukhoy Babu had told us this is his property. He made us promises of big donations and land. We foolishly believed him. Alas, we holy people do not know the ways of the material world. We are too trusting. You seem like a good man. And your wife is the incarnate of Goddess Lakshmi. My blessings be with you two, always.'

'Thank you!'

Even the way he turned the ignition on told me that he was seething.

'Nikhil?'

'Please leave me alone for a while.'

I turned and looked out of the window trying not to feel miserable.

I wasn't speaking to him to ask for something for myself. I was just trying to comfort him. Why did he need to snap? What had I done? Yet, if I didn't understand him, who would? I know the strains he had been through in the past year. I knew just how rotten and demanding the business had been all of this past week. After all of that he is entitled to a little space. So was I crowding him? Was he feeling stifled?

While these thoughts flitted through my mind, I was absently twisting the ring on my finger.

'It is at times like these that you sorely wish you could take that ring off and fling it at me.'

I looked at him. He still looked grim, but I knew he wasn't that angry any more. I wrinkled my nose at him.

'Come sit with me, Bula.'

He held out his left hand. I moved close to him. At traffic lights when we needed to wait, his thumb massaged the side of my neck. And we sat in perfect silence.

✦

We went to this large medical college and hospital at Sealdah. Chaudhuri Kaku was standing on the edge of a crowd at the porch, all looking lost. He came forward seeing Nikhil.

'Here, take care of this for me.'

Nikhil thrust out a back pack at me.

Chaudhuri Kaku said that the doctor on duty had still not seen his daughter yet. She was in the casualty room. Inside the room, the mother sat holding Indrani's limp hand. Indrani seemed semi-conscious. Her two brothers, Atanu and Shantanu stood in the corridor outside not really sure what to do.

Thankfully a doctor came in then and shooed us all away. After examining Indrani he spoke to us. He explained that he was the Resident Medical Officer. On preliminary examination it seemed like a neurological complaint. The Neurologist came only thrice a week and was on call for emergencies but the fees would be high. He recommended that the patient be admitted immediately so that proper medical attention could be provided.

Then Nikhil took over. From the bag he had given me, he took two thick bundles of currency notes and went towards the admission counter. He filled the necessary documents and completed the admission formalities and even had the Neurologist summoned. He had secured a very comfortable private room with a wide bed for an attendant. He personally made sure that Indrani was immediately and comfortably settled into the room. He found a doctor on duty and got him to come and attend to her. While he was running around organising all the needed to be done, I sat with the distraught Mrs. Chaudhuri who wanted to recount what had happened.

On Friday evening, Indrani's husband and in-laws brought her back along with her year-old baby girl. They fought with the Chaudhuris for having palmed off an unfit and sick girl as a burden on them. It was only then that the parents found out that for over the past year she used to throw up, complain of unbearable headaches and have frequent fainting spells.

While her husband and in-laws were shouting and screaming she just sat mute watching it all unfold, taking in all the abuses without flinching. She was silent but alright till late this afternoon when she suddenly went into what looked like an epileptic fit and then just settled into this semi-conscious state.

Her mother began weeping then. I tried to comfort her, the best I could.

The Neurologist's visit simply confirmed that it was indeed a neurological complaint. He would prescribe something to stabilise her through the night. But he needed extensive tests in order to pinpoint that exact illness. And all of that could only be done during the day time.

The parents wanted to stay with her through the night.

'Nikhil Babu, you will have to give me leave for a few days,' Chaudhuri Kaka turned to him.

'Of course, Kaka. I will be here by eight-thirty in the morning and be with you till the tests all get done.'

'No Nikhil Babu, there is too much work these days. I will manage. I will tell Shantanu to come and help me. Atanu will go to the godown as usual. You have already done so much. I couldn't have done the admission and all without your help.'

'You leave that to me, Kaka. Come,' he said to the boys, 'I'll drop you home.'

During the drive he chatted with the boys enquiring where Indrani's little daughter was and whether they had dinner ready for them. It seems their other sister had been married into a family in the neighbourhood and she was helping out with the baby and the food for the family. We dropped them off outside her gates.

'Nikhil, please stop the car.'

He found a spot beside the road and parked there. It was pitch black outside. I reached out and brought his head to my chest and held him. I stroked his hair trying to help him forget the weirdness of the day, and slowly he stroked me back on my hands, my neck, my sides....

By the time we reached home it was almost eleven thirty. A bleary eyed Sraboni served us dinner together in the dining hall. Both of us were too tired to eat but ate mechanically anyway.

'Had Kishore-da left?' Nikhil asked.

'Yes, there were many scenes of shouting and tears. But Akhil Dada just stood there and made sure he left telling him that if you wanted him out, there was no way in the world that he could continue to stay.'

'I see. Sraboni, on other days I know Bula arranges things and washes up. From now on it is your duty to see that it's done.'

'Yes, Dada.'

We went up together. He didn't even go to his room to change but came in with me and lay down on the bed.

'I'll go get your pyjamas. I think it's unhygienic to sleep in your jeans.'

'Let it be, Bula. I am really dead. Come, put me to sleep.'

He held me around the waist, snuggled in and fell asleep soon.

+ + +

29

Bula: 29 years

I was in the kitchen a little before six on the next morning deciding what needed to be bought and done for lunch and dinner. Breakfast preparations were underway. Nikhil came in. He stood beside me.

'Please give very precise instructions to Sraboni and come up with me. Sujoya please have breakfast ready for Bula and me in half an hour's time. We both have to go to office today.'

This was the first time I had come to Nikhil's office. It was a smart two-storeyed building. Downstairs there was a huge hall with numerous desks, lined on one-side with cubicles. Upstairs, where there were many rooms, he took me to one with a glass door and which bore his name in gold on it – Nikhil Mitra. He led me inside.

'Bula, for this week you will need to fill up for me. I wish I could spare you this. But with both Chaudhuri Kaku and me away, only you can help us. Are you up to it?'

The enormity of it hit me then and I felt numb. I nodded still.

The next hour Nikhil explained a lot of work-related matters to me. Some I knew. Some I was slightly familiar with. Others were completely new concepts altogether.

'Look, I'll try and call you as often as possible from some phone in the hospital. If you cannot take a decision, or want to discuss it once with me, just wait for my call. Okay?'

'Yes, Nikhil.'

'I'm sorry, Bula, I have to rush now. I want to be in the hospital in half an hour's time. People will begin to come in by nine. Lynette can help you with some of the paperwork. In case you need clarification, get hold of Parvez. I will try and come to pick you up. If I can't, I'll make sure Dhanraj will take you home.'

I caught a mild glow as his eyes studied me.

'All the best, on your first day in office! It's a very proud moment for me, Bula. Too bad I can't stay and savour it.'

It took me over two months to be aware of what I was really doing. Thankfully in all that time I made no big mistakes and Nikhil was almost always accessible to guide me. The way the company had been set up and with the people Nikhil had hand-picked and trained, it ran like an efficient organisation, even in his absence.

Further tests on Indrani had confirmed the earlier suspicion that she had a tumour in her brain. The doctors recommended that she be taken to CMC at Vellore, the country's best facility, as the tumour had progressed and required an immediate operation. Chaudhuri Kaku turned to Nikhil again. And Nikhil stood by him like a pillar of strength. In seven days time, with all the appointments fixed on the phone; Nikhil, Indrani, Chaudhuri Kaku and Atanu flew down to Madras and went on to Vellore. Nikhil stayed in Vellore for four days until the operation was conducted and declared successful. Indrani needed a recuperation period of three weeks and if progress permitted, she would travel back to Kolkata.

While he was in Vellore, Nikhil would call me late every evening and talk for a long time. I would wait for his call beside the telephone in his study.

'How has your day been? Missed me?'

'My day has been okay mostly. Didn't miss you much. You've dumped too much work on me for me to do.'

'Hey, don't do the work. That's optional. But you simply have to miss me.'

'Why?'

'I don't want to be the only one to.'

'Oh Nikhil, I miss you terribly. The house feels haunted without you. Never go away again.'

'You know I had to do this. Chaudhuri Kaku is a family member now and needed me. Time passes during the day as we all have a lot of running around to do. But when I come back to my room to sleep, it's unbearable. I can't sleep without you by my side anymore.'

'At least you are in a strange room. Here everything I see reminds me of you. Everything is the same as it always was, but without you they all seem strange and hostile somehow. Missing you is not a nice feeling, Nikhil.'

'Poor Bula! The good part is that I should be home by day after tomorrow. And when I come I'll take one whole day off and just spend it with you. I'll just lie in your arms all day.'

'The amount of work that is pending will not permit you that luxury.'

'Will you?'

'Only if you promise to let me lie in yours part of the time.'

'I'd like nothing better.'

'Nikhil, are you eating alright?'

'I eat with the others and normally I ask them to order for me as well. But I miss my tea.'

'Why can't you be like the millions others and go buy yourself some?'

'I'm addicted to a particular kind of tea.'

'Yes. But in a situation like this when that is not possible?'

'I drink coffee instead.'

As I had foreseen, we did not get to spend that day together on his return. There was simply too much work. However at breakfast Nikhil asked me how my experiences at office had been. I filled him in the best I could.

'Bula, this was your trial period. In this time, the office next door which used to be Bankim Kaku's has been readied for you. I would like you to come to office everyday or as often as it is possible for you.'

'I'd like that.'

'The work is growing. You have seen how complex and demanding it is. I can't do it alone. I don't want to anymore. Right now, I really need you.'

'I'll get ready and come down soon.'

The office next door was identical to his. A new glass door bore my name – Bula Banerjee.

'That's my maiden name. How did you know?'

'There's very little I don't know about you, Bula.'

I explored my new office. There was a connecting door to Nikhil's office. Everything I may need was laid out on my desk. Even the swivel chair had been adjusted to my height. There was a large window that looked out onto a small back garden. I stood behind the closed window looking out. Nikhil came and stood behind me.

'Everything all right?'

I nodded.

'I have wanted this for a very long time, Bula. I wanted you to have work worthy of you and your capabilities and not the menial tasks set for you at home. I gave you time to grow into this naturally. Right from the first day of accounting, this is what I had envisioned for you. Finally I feel it has all paid off. And the bonus for me is that I will have you by my side all day.'

We left office around five. Nikhil drove into an unfamiliar road in a busy shopping area and found us a parking spot. We entered a huge snazzy saree shop. There was a pleasant-looking young man behind the counter who smiled at us politely in greeting and then, as he registered Nikhil, his jaw dropped.

'Mitra, bugger, is that you?'

He came out from behind the counter and hugged Nikhil hard.

'Where the hell have you been all this time?'

'Hey man! Nice to see you, too. Been here and there, mostly busy. Bula, meet Mehul. He was with me at college.'

Mehul shouted out to his wife Gunjan at the far end of the store.

'My wife, Gunjan. This is Nikhil Mitra, my college *yaar*, and his wife, Bula.'

Nikhil put an arm around me casually. Then he said something he would always repeat in situations like this.

'Bula is not my wife, though I wish she also was. She is far more important, my business partner.'

Then turning to Gunjan with a smile he asked, 'Could you help Bula choose a few sarees? We are both clueless.'

As Gunjan led me away to a counter deeper in the store, Mehul was calling someone on the phone, excitedly.

'Faltu, you won't imagine who is in my store right now. Hang your meeting, bugger, Just come. It's big, I tell you.'

'Would you like to see something traditional or fancy?'

'Traditional, I think.'

Gunjan assisted by a couple of sales girls spent an hour educating me on the various traditional weaves. The shopping trip had been a surprise and I was unsure what I wanted to buy and how many I would need. In the end I settled for five semi-formal sarees, one for each day of the work week. I chose two voiles with chikankari work and three woven sarees including an exquisite Bangla taat.

When I was done I looked around for Nikhil and he was holding a soft drink bottle, laughing and talking to Mehul and two other men, evidently classmates. He looked relaxed and a lot younger. I guess reminiscing with old friends does that to you. He looked in my direction. He raised his bottle a little as an intimate salute. Something soft and radiant came into his gaze and made me feel warm from within.

'Done?'

'I think so.'

'Come here. Meet these other jokers from my college days. This is Faltu and that is not just his name, it's an apt description.'

That earned Nikhil a thump on his back.

'Man, why are you doing this to me in front of Bou-di? I am Fali Tarapore.'

He shook my hand.

'And I am Arindam Dasgupta.'

'Bugger, do you still play football?'

'No I grew up, unlike you juveniles.'

'Bou-di, does he write poetry to you? He used to write all our love letters.'

'Why don't you even show up at our parties, Mitra?'

'Gentlemen, I do not lead the frivolous life of leisure you do.'

'Bug off. You think we don't keep tabs on you. You are making crores in a week, man. You can buy all the leisure in the world.'

Nikhil smiled a wry smile and I knew he had been made acutely aware of all the things missing in his life his money couldn't buy. A couple of invitations were pressed on Nikhil. Everyone exchanged cards and then we simply had to leave.

As it happened, Gunjan took upon herself the habit of sending across to the office a selection of sarees every couple of months. We'd drop by that evening and pay for the lot. It became a kind of social ritual.

In the car I asked him:

'Did you seriously write love letters and poetry?'

He looked at me with a smile.

'What do you think?'

'I think I have been cheated out of some things.'

'Love letters and poetry are just words, Bula. That is easy to do, especially when the object is imaginary.'

'Do you mean it is tough being in love with a flesh and blood object?'

'Don't you?'

I felt a little hurt at the implication that it was difficult for him to love me.

'I don't mean being in love. I mean expressing that love anew each day and building on it so that it remains young and fresh and valid. It is so easy to take each other for granted.'

'But anybody would naturally express what they feel.'

'It does not always happen naturally. There are people who are normally reticent and the people they love don't know how much they care.'

'What about you?'

He took a while to think it over.

'I think, Bula, I have not been able to successfully communicate just how much I love you and how much you mean to me. I try; almost in every thought, word and action. Yet there are things from the normal rhythm of life – work, circumstances, other people, and my own nature – all of which waylay me from what is central to my life. You.'

The words were hard for him to articulate. I could see the effort it was taking him.

'Men and women love differently, Bula. Men demand so much. At each step I have taken you further from your comfort zone and you willingly gave in to each of my demands. It is not that I don't realise just how tough it is to overcome a mindset or a system of values. And for each demand of mine you set aside your inner voice and gave in to me gladly. That trust, that belief in my vision and the unquestioning surrender to it, is a very rare form of love, Bula. I have stood in one place. And you have made this long arduous journey to come to me. And now that you are with me, sometimes I cannot tell, where I end and you begin.'

I turned to him, my eyes shining.

'If anything I have done and still do makes you happy or enhances your life. It makes my life worthwhile.'

'I wish I was not driving right now. Then I could have kissed you thoroughly as you so richly deserve right now.'

I rested my head on his shoulder feeling very contented.

'Thank you for taking me shopping today! It was not as stressful as I had feared it would be. And I liked all your friends.'

'Yeah, this trip was long overdue. I'm glad you liked them. They are all good guys.'

We went together to meet my mother-in-law. She had shrunk and aged further since Aukhoy Babu was sent away.

'You were asleep when we left, Ranga Ma. I hope you are well. Today was a very significant day. Bula has started going to office on a regular basis.'

She raised very sad eyes at him.

'Nikhil, you don't know how much I have dreamed of this for Kishore. He never did it. Never did anything I advised him to. And today I don't even know where my son is.'

'Let him lead his own life, Ranga Ma. You can't lead it for him.'

Nikhil sat beside her and held her hand comfortingly.

'Please find him for me and bring him back.'

'I may do that for you some day. But now he needs to sort himself out and I don't think living here was helping him do that.'

'Your mother was so blessed that she had a son like you, Nikhil. All of them are in the same house, similar circumstances, same food.... Only you turned out this way.'

Then she turned towards me.

'Bou-ma, no woman from this household or any related one has ever left home to go to work. I don't understand why you need to. So don't expect me to be happy that you are going to work. But I also realise that what I think and feel, what I have seen and known so far, will all be outdated. Now the world belongs to others, it's not my say anymore. Do what you both think is best.'

✦ ✦ ✦

30

Bula: 30 years

Working alongside Nikhil was an exhilarating experience. I had imagined that the nature of his responsibilities would render him a demanding boss. On extremely rare occasions when the pressure was off, Nikhil would be silent, keep low and let the office regulate itself. When things got demanding, he would work tirelessly alongside his team, encouraging them and leading by example. It was in moments of crisis that Nikhil was at his superlative best. He would sort out the issue with patience and clear thinking. He would be at his most humorous and talkative then, easing the stress and nervousness all around.

It was evident that everyone in the office absolutely adored Nikhil. No one behaved like a salaried employee, rather like a friend sworn to serve him.

With me, he was like a dream. I had been a little wary about how my being in office would affect his functioning and our relationship. Nikhil's attitude allayed all my fears. He made this smooth transformation from colleague to lover and back again in a swift unselfconscious sweep.

We would be discussing something important and he would be asking me pertinent questions.

'And how do you justify a five lakhs expenditure on a new godown when trucks from the existing godown seven kilometers away can well service that area?'

And while I would marshal my objectives for this proposal, he'd smile mischievously and lean forward to kiss me passionately before resuming the discussion. I'd be left grasping for words. In meetings with others he would be focused and hard-headed. Then for a long moment his eyes would rest on me, turn liquid with love, and suddenly he would go back to the speaker with another incisive question.

'Without a scientific sales projection for that area, what is your company's basis for recommending to us that we take up distribution there?'

People in the office knew me as Bankim Babu's daughter-in-law. And they were all extremely protective of Nikhil. I would have preferred not to offend their sensibilities by making explicit the relationship Nikhil and I shared.

However, right from my first day at office Nikhil chose to be demonstrative and open, genuinely happy that I was there with him. Whenever he stood beside me, he would put his arm around me and hold me close. He always held my hand protectively when I used the stairs. In his smile, the way he looked at me, or teased me, there were the unmistakable signs of love. Even the tone in which he addressed me was intimate and unambiguous.

His message to all in the office seemed to be:

'Clearly we are together. It may not fit in with your ideas or values. Deal with it. If you respect and love me, I would like you to now extend the same to this inseparable part of my life.'

Some time back Nikhil had won an award and I found an album with professional photographs from the awards function. There was one of Nikhil accepting the award from the wife of the Industries Minister. He was smiling up at her shyly and in that shot the photographer seemed to have serendipitously captured the essence of Nikhil. I asked to have the picture enlarged and framed and it hung on a wall across my desk so that I just needed to lift my gaze and see Nikhil if my work day ever got beyond me.

And that it rarely did. It was the atmosphere in the office. It was the nurture and the grounding Nikhil had painstakingly given me over the years. It was the desire that had awakened in me to prove myself and justify Nikhil's decision to have me as a partner. I threw myself passionately into my work; sometimes unable to see it as distinct from my love for Nikhil.

Working together afforded us many opportunities to be closer. There were times when we would sit in either office, silently going through documents or financial statements that needed our attention. I would feel Nikhil's gaze at the top of my head. I'd look up. He would look at me seriously and unblinkingly. I'd smile. I'd reach out and touch his face. And he would close his eyes and breathe deep.

'What's up, Nikhil?' I'd ask.

In reply he would just smile a slow heartfelt smile. It would be my turn to catch my breath.

When we needed to work late, he would insist we take a break from work. Sometimes we would just go for a short brisk walk or drive down to a nearby park and sit on the bench, talking. Often we would go down to the back garden and sit there sipping tea I'd prepare. Once he saw me wince straightening up in my chair. He began this ritual of massaging my shoulder once a day during which it was off limits to discuss or think of work at all.

Over the years Nikhil had slowly and inexorably given a little more of himself to me at each step. The only part of Nikhil that I hadn't been familiar with was his persona at work. And now he had shared even that with me. Knowing him to be reticent and private by nature, I knew just how deep his trust in me would have been to reveal and share so much of himself. I now had an intimate view of all of him. It was as attractive, as beautiful as the Nikhil I had always known.

✦

The next crisis that our household had to tackle came very soon. We were all at dinner save for the girls who had been fed and put to sleep in preparation for school the next day.

Ajit looked at his mother guardedly and then turned to Nikhil.

'Nikhil-da, Amit and I have something to ask of you.'

'Go ahead.'

He gave his mother another look.

'We have both been applying to universities in the US for our B.S. degree. Both of us have been accepted at a place called Rensselaer Polytechnic in New York State. It is a very credible place.'

'That's very good. Congrats!'

'You can't go abroad to study,' their mother cut in.

'Let him speak, Ranga Ma. Let's hear them out.'

Amit spoke up now.

'We have secured admission and a part-waiver of the tuition fees. Still the hostel and living expenses will be whopping.'

'No question of your going then,' my mother-in-law snapped.

'Do you and Ajit really want to go?' Nikhil asked them.

'It's only a matter of money,' they replied together.

'Don't worry about the money. Just be very sure that it is really what you want. Adjusting to life in a foreign country is quite tough. And the academics will be different and demanding too.'

'We really want to go, Nikhil-da.'

'Why are you even listening to this nonsense, Nikhil? They will study here and then join the business.'

'Everyone has dreams, Ranga Ma. Maybe theirs is this.'

'What about my dreams? I want all my children around me. As it is you have banished my Kishore. And now you will be sending these little ones away....'

'Ma, Nikhil-da will not be sending us, but sponsoring us instead. He can choose not to. But Amit and I will try again until we can make it. You all can delay our going or make it difficult, but go we will.'

'What about me? What about your responsibilities to your poor widowed mother?'

'Frankly, Ma, neither of us can take better care of you than Nikhil-da has taken all these days. We want to be there for you. But we want to make our lives better for ourselves as well. And this is very important to us.'

'What do you think, Bula?'

I didn't want to reply. Finally I said:

'The twins are grown up now. We cannot tie them down. As a family we should support them in all their positive endeavours.'

'You don't talk at all! Has anyone been able to tie you down? You have been doing exactly what you want all these days,' my mother-in-law turned to me angrily.

'Precisely, Ma. It is just impossible to try and tie anybody down. It is just a matter of three years. They can always come back and join the business in future.'

My mother-in-law began to cry then. Nikhil looked at her, a little upset at her tears. Then he spoke to the twins.

'Since I have taken up the running of the business, I have tried my best to make sure every need of my family is taken care of. Money will not be a problem for either of you. However, you will need to convince Ranga Ma and gain her consent first.'

'How much do you think it will cost? Akhil asked.

'We are not sure. But it could be around one and a half to four lakhs per person in three years.'

'That's a lot of money!' Akhil exclaimed.

'How does the amount matter, Akhil? You know that we can afford it,' Nikhil said.

'No, Dada, I am thinking in terms of return on investment. They could easily study at a top college in the country for a tenth of that amount. Is it worth going abroad just on a whim?'

'Akhil, the concept of returns on investments does not apply to dreams. I refuse to consider the twins' future in terms of capital and gains.'

After that, dinner was a glum affair. Everyone was caught in their own thoughts.

That night, Nikhil was very quiet.

'Bula, the house will get even emptier without the twins.'

'Yes, Nikhil. Yet you must set them free one day. That is the nature of bringing up children.'

'I can see Ranga Ma's point of view too. But I don't want to stand in the way of their future.'

'It will sort itself out. Don't worry about it.'

'Do you worry about the girls?'

'All the time.'

'Why don't you tell me about your worries then?'

'Right now they are idle worries. When they get more concrete, I'll share them with you.'

He kept silent for a while. Then he touched my forehead lightly.

'Bula, do you ever feel like going away to fulfill your dreams?'

'My dreams have all been fulfilled, Nikhil.'

'What if you have new dreams?'

'Then I promise you that none of them will involve my going away. And all of them will always include you.'

'How can you be so sure?'

'I just am.'

✦

The twins left home. My mother-in-law was prevailed upon to give her consent.

One day Akhil and Niru caught us off-guard. They made us a very cogent presentation of a business proposal. They wanted the company to invest in a night club that the two of them would run. Nikhil, the big-hearted softie was never likely to deny any member of his family anything. I would always concur with Nikhil. But if either of us needed to be won over, the power of the presentation and the realisation that the pair of them were finally thinking of gainful occupation would have influenced us heavily.

Ever since Digha, Akhil and Niru assimilated more into the family. Akhil especially had grown very close. He would seek me out each day and spend some time talking to me. He tended to hug me or lie down with his big head on my lap behaving as a much-loved younger brother. Then he had this insatiable appetite for home-made sweets that no one really made anymore and would put in steady requests and I would try and make as many varieties of them as I could. At meal times he would be animated, the life and soul at the table, while also keeping tabs on how little I ate and scolding me.

Even Nikhil noticed this change.

'Akhil seems so much closer to you these days.'

'Yes; earlier he used to see me as Aukhoy Babu's wife.'

'And now?'

'Now he feels attached to me because of you.'

Another noticeable trait in Akhil was that he turned fiercely protective of Nikhil and me. His handling of Aukhoy Babu and his questioning the twins about expenses was his way of making sure that Nikhil's softness and generosity was not exploited by anyone.

Niru Babu finally decided to get married. All of us visited Krishnanagar on a Saturday evening to attend the reception at his parent's house. After Niru's departure, Akhil moped around the house for a couple of weeks and then went back to partying with his usual crowd. In a couple of months, Niru was back. He has stayed with us ever since. He visits his family for about three or four days in a month. Other than that he is a permanent fixture.

Akhil and Niru shortlisted various sites and settled on a fantastic location for the nightclub. Nikhil insisted on buying the property rather than renting; considering the latter a more unstable business model and unnecessary given that funds were available. The real estate prices were killing but that upscale locality also made it an even more profitable investment. At Akhil's request, Nikhil and I performed the *bhoomi* puja prior to construction at the site.

For the next year Akhil would drive us mad thrusting various photographs, fabric and colour samples and glossy design books at us, asking us to choose between a few selected options. We would all sit together and hammer it out until we reached a consensus. Choosing a name for the place was another activity that all of us collaborated in. It was an unspoken belief though that Nikhil's choice would be the final one.

Dinners for that whole year meant that the four of us would only talk about the nightclub. On the rare occasions my mother-in-law joined us, she would protest and Nikhil always dutiful, would turn contrite and apologise to her and banish the discussion from the table for that night.

One night however he spoke up hesitantly.

'Ranga Ma, I'm sorry. But this is important. Please bear with me.'

Then turning to us all he said:

'I've been wondering. We have a prime property in a great locality. Why keep it shut until eight every evening? In effect we are only running it for three hours every night and earning revenues for only that brief period.'

'Dada, at the rates we are planning to charge and the cover costs and all, it will all work out. Besides just three hours of work for us each night is precisely the attractive bit about this proposition.'

'Why don't we run it as a breakfast, snack and coffee bar till seven in the evening and close it for an hour and then open at eight as a nightclub?'

We stared at him stunned. The work and the turnaround required would increase manifold. He won us over with very convincing statistics though. Then we all got into the spirit of things. The walls were all to be painted in versatile paint that looked plain in the day and turned psychedelic under special neon lights. Now we needed two sets of light fittings to go with each mood. Four additional staff members would have to be hired just to effect that change every evening and again after closing each night. Akhil and Niru slogged unflaggingly to make this happen.

The only time I have been to the Passionflower was with the entire family – Ma, kids and all, for the inauguration. That day it was a simple tame affair of meeting lots of colleagues, friends and relatives.

Ever since, the place has a reputation of a hot, desired destination in town. It is a regular haunt for painters, actors, poets, models, rich kids, corporate types and even the underworld. Many rock bands got their big break playing on the stage here. It is rumoured that the nightclub does not close for the night at all but transitions smoothly into a breakfast and coffee haunt for all those who party hard through the night. And all this is blessed and enabled by a young group of politicians who choose to spend their nights there.

Akhil began to have a string of beauties come into his life. He seriously dated each of them for a few months and then moved on to the next. I teased him about them. Nikhil would get concerned and advise him to choose someone he liked and settle down. Akhil would answer wearily.

'Dada, in this city all I seem to find are Reba clones. And of all people in the world, you should understand.'

Nikhil still regretted how empty the house seemed ever since the twins had left. He began persuading Niru to bring his wife to stay with us. Even the mention of the topic made Niru pale. He was perfectly happy with his hard partying lifestyle and long distance marriage.

In time, Akhil and Niru felt confident about their capabilities and opted to plough back profits and take another handout from the company to open a restaurant on the terrace of the building. After months of brainstorming we chose a hothouse restaurant. It was to be called The Garden of Eden. The idea of eating in a lush garden among exotic tropical plants under a glass ceiling was unique and this venture too was a huge success.

✦ ✦ ✦

31

Bula: 20 years

I was going for my Rabindra Sangeet lessons at Jharna's house. Ashu was standing at the small, side gate that led straight to the mango orchards. I had dreamt of this so often since he had left for the US that I wrote this off as another phantasm.

'Bula!'

This was unmistakably Ashu's voice. I looked up still fearing this was a dream. He was waving frantically at me.

'Ashu! When did you come?'

'I just came to India last night and this afternoon I rushed to Phuleshwar to see you.'

I almost ran to the gate as he spoke. He let me in. And once the mango trees shielded us from the road, he took me in his arms and bent down to kiss me. The past twenty months of longing seeped through me and I held him delicately, kissing him back with all my heart.

'Oh, Bula! It feels so good to hold you.'

My eyes burned with joy.

'I have actually come to invite you to Calcutta. Do you think your mother would give you permission to come away with me for ten days?'

I didn't think my mother would. But I would go to the ends of the world to be with Ashu.

'Bula, I'm getting married.'

I stared at him, uncomprehending. He chattered on, not really noticing.

'She is my Kolkata college professor's daughter. You remember she had come to Case Western too, to study Philosophy. Her name is Saswati. You would love her.'

And then he noticed my thunderstruck face.

'Why Bula, what happened?'

I hurried to rearrange my expressions with a wan smile.

'No, nothing.'

'You are happy for me, aren't you? You know for the longest time in the world I just wanted to marry you. It's funny how intense everything is when you are growing up.... You still are the only friend I have in Phuleshwar. My best buddy.'

He smiled happily and looked around.

'Nothing changes in this place. It is still in that same old slow pace. Time just seems to stand still here.'

'Yeah, including me,' I thought bitterly.

'Ashu, I am getting late for my class. I need to go.'

'No, spend this hour with me, Bula. For old time's sake'

He leaned forward and kissed my mouth again. I almost weakened. But I pushed him away and wiped my lips.

'You shouldn't be doing that.'

'Why? Bula, I still love you. That doesn't change and it never will.'

I just turned blindly and ran out of the mango orchard then. I ran all the way to class. When I reached Jharna's house all hot and breathless, I just sat on the verandah. I was a little late. Class had started. My teacher, Aurobindo Sir, was performing a perfect rendition of '*Purano sey deener kotha...*' (The tales of those days gone by).

I just broke down and wept, finally realising how wretched I really was.

✦ ✦ ✦

32

Bula: 32 years

The children's school had a function that Saturday morning. Both the girls were in the dances of their age groups. The mothers of the participants had been requested to come and help out backstage, particularly with costume and make-up. My girls were so sweet and accommodating of my heavy work schedule that I wanted to be there for them.

The program ended around twelve. I left the school premises holding the girls by their wrists as they squirmed about shouting farewells to their friends.

'Bula!' Sharmishtha, a neighbour whose daughter was a classmate called out. 'Do you know that one of your brothers-in-law has had a massive accident this morning?'

I stared at her uncomprehending.

'The one who drives the black Ambassador. A drunken truck driver just mowed into his car.'

It was Nikhil. I couldn't move.

'Bula, are you alright?'

'It's my Nikhil!'

I spotted Dhanraj.

'Dhanraj. Home.'

'Why are you crying, Bou-di?'

I couldn't tell him.

As the car drew to the gate I just jumped off and ran into our compound. The extreme right corner of the front corridor had a large doorway into what used to be Tarapada Babu's cavernous bedroom. A huge crowd stood along the corridor, almost blocking the entrance. I ran past everybody and stood at the doorway of the packed room.

Nikhil was alive!

His head was bandaged heavily around the crown and I could see some patches of dull brown medicine having seeped on to the white gauze. His left arm and leg were unnaturally bulky under the white sheet covering him so I knew they were in casts. I stood there bewildered, staring, unable to acknowledge that he was hurt and joyous that he was alive.

Everyone remotely connected to us was there. My mother-in-law sat in a straight-backed chair, her head covered demurely among the crowds of men. Sharmishtha came in behind me and so did the kids. I was oblivious to it all. I stood drinking my fill of Nikhil. His eyes were on the doorway. Seeing me, he smiled a tired, tight smile. He raised his right hand a little, reaching out to me. I ran to his bed and sat down to his right.

For a fraction of a second the hordes of acquaintances and my mother-in-law's gimlet eyes held me back. Then I lay down lightly on Nikhil's chest. His arm came up around me holding me tight.

'I didn't know. I'm so sorry. I'm sorry I wasn't there.'

'It's okay. Don't cry,' he whispered.

'Are you okay?'

'I feel tired. But I'm fine.'

I lifted myself up a fraction till my face was inches from his. We looked at each other as if for the first time in years. His hand touched my cheek and rested there lightly. We spoke in whispers.

'Thank God you weren't in the car today.'

'I should have been with you.'

'No Bula. Thank God you weren't.'

'Can I get you anything?'

His arm tightened a bit.

'Everything I need, I have.'

My eyes filled up with tears. He touched my eye with a fingertip.

'If you cry, it hurts even more.'

'I won't if you promise to get better soon.'

'I will. For you.'

'Your lips look dry. Shall I get you some water?'

'Just give me a spoonful.'

There was a glass of water on the table beside the bed. I found a spoon too and moist his lips with a spoonful of water. He closed his eyes.

Akhil came up and held me then. I buried my face in his shirt and began to sob.

'Bou-di, Dada is fine.'

'Akhil, why isn't Nikhil in hospital getting proper medical care?'

'He is not that badly hurt. The greater impact was on the passenger side. He is fine really. They did all the tests and then discharged him. He only needs painkillers and rest now.'

I raised a teary face to him.

'How can you be sure?'

'The doctors are very sure, Bou-di.'

'Akhil, can you ask all these people to leave. He will need his rest.'

'Sure Bou-di.'

Nikhil opened his eyes again and looked at me. I leaned towards him, stroking his face.

'Nikhil, get some rest.'

'Bula, don't leave me now.'

I held his hand softly in both of mine.

'I won't, Nikhil. Never again!'

I would sit on the bed beside him hoping to be there when he came awake. His eyes would flutter open and seeing me, he would smile.

I would blink back tears. I would lean forward and kiss him, the accident having completely stripped me of self-consciousness, even in the presence of Akhil, Niru or the kids.

'How are you feeling now?'

'Happy.'

Akhil would sit and regale us, when the kids were at school, with his take on the dramatic scene of my entry into the room that day.

'Niru, it was straight out of the second last reel of a Hindi film. Heroine comes to the door quivering. Hero looks up weakly. Heroine runs to his bedside.'

'Shut up, Akhil. Show Bula some respect.'

'Heroine flings herself into hero's arms. Hero holds her close. I look around the room. The average population is above sixty years old. How many heart attacks? If it happens within our premises are we liable to pay out compensation? Ranga Ma flip-flops on the verge of an apoplectic fit.'

'Really? I didn't notice.'

'How would you notice, Bou-di? You were completely absorbed by our hero then and have always been as far back as I can remember.'

Nikhil drew my hand over his heart.

'Then I told myself, all these weirdoes are a pain anyway. So we will have some bit of collateral damages. Let our happy couple have a joyful reunion – you know songs, dance, rainbows, doves and all. Still I think I should limit the amount of that damage especially when I am thinking cold hard cash and liability and compensation and all; and so I hold Bou-di. Of course I had to practically wrench her away from Dada. Man has no sense of propriety in public.'

'Akhil, shut up!'

'No, really Dada, all these doddering old men in the room and you are shamelessly whispering to your lady love. *Tch tch*. Anyway to come back to the masala storyline, I hold Bou-di. Bou-di clings to me and cries. Junta is perplexed. Now who is this villain? And before any answers come, villain true to his nature starts shooing people out and denying them further entertainment.'

'Are you done?'

Akhil would smile at his adored older brother teasingly.

'Don't blush, Dada. Yours is a beautiful love story. You are a lucky man!'

Nikhil got serious then. His hand drew me down until we looked into each other's eyes. He spoke out loud enough for everyone in the room but his eyes spoke only to me.

'You know, after the crash for a while I lost consciousness. I only came awake with medication and was very fuzzy. Bula, I couldn't remember whether you were in the car with me. You are with me every day. And I recalled you sitting there beside me, smiling up at me. I knew the truck had come into that side. Somewhere I seemed to recall seeing you being caught in that crumpling mess of metal. I was so strongly sedated, Bula, that I couldn't keep awake. But I stayed staring at the door, hoping against hope that those images were just my fevered imagination. And then you appeared at the doorway, beautiful, vibrant. I held out my hand, telling you: if you are just a spectre take me with you and if you are alive, come to me. Until I held you, Bula, I wasn't sure whether I would ever hold you again.'

He held me then. We were lost in each other for a long time and then we heard Niru say.

'Come, Akhil, let's take a cigarette break.'

Nikhil looked up.

'So Akhil you have taken up smoking after all.'

'No, Dada. Why does Akhil need cigarettes? What cigarettes do for me, he was a harem of beauties to take care of.'

'You don't talk, okay? You know, Bou-di every year a calendar is printed in the Datta household. How does that happen? Artificial insemination?'

'Akhil-Niru, will you guys go now? Go, smoke grass for all I care as long as Bula and I don't have to put up with this conversation....'

✦ ✦ ✦

33

Bula: 34 years

Rains turned into winters and winters broke out into spring song. The years turned. And yet the love and its bliss endured.

Sometimes I wondered why Nikhil and I never had fights or disputes that couples are supposed to. Wondered too, whether that is what the future would bring and would threaten to disrupt or destroy all that we had. Yet every night was sweet. Every morning waking to each other was as powerful as prayer. I needed to go down to the kitchens very early to flag off the day with instructions. Nikhil woke up for a bit then and we'd lie together talking in low voices. And while I tackled the day's work schedule and menu, I'd think ahead to going up with his morning tea and waking him again.

We truly had our peaceful microcosm. On days I realised just how fortunate I was, I would even thank my experiences with Aukhoy Babu for teaching me the importance of peaceful and respectful coexistence. It was like we'd braved the worst storms and now preferred to rest among rainbows. And with work and everything else poised the way it was, having each other was the greatest gift, the greatest joy.

Out of the blue, Reba wrote a long letter to Nikhil. Sadly Reba the actress, did not happen. Her largest contribution to the great world of Bangla cinema comprised five risqué dances that made her name synonymous with oomph. It seems she tired of being a vamp and decided to turn producer and relaunched herself as a heroine. Audiences have long term memory and rebranding one's image is not as easy as it sounds. The film tanked badly and Reba now had blood-thirsty creditors at her door. She needed a lot of money and failing everywhere else had decided to impinge on Nikhil's generosity. The amount was really too large to be given without bleeding. That predisposed Nikhil to wash his hands off it all. I however advised Nikhil that this was a perfect opportunity for him to negotiate for a full custody of Tathagata in return. While neither our business nor our personal accounts could yield that much money without serious difficulty, with careful management we were in a position to raise the money. Of course it was a risk. I felt it was all worth it for the pay off I visualised. Perhaps in hindsight those expensive lawyers were an indulgence, but I wanted the deal to be watertight. Reba was in such straits that she was only too glad to sign anywhere in order to get the money. That we were asking for Tathagata with generous visitation rights for her may have seemed like a bonus to her. For us it was a dream come true.

He was a little older than ten when he came to stay with us. He was an unnaturally quiet child who would just sit and watch everything around him with large watery eyes.

Something about him reminded me of Nikhil when I had first met him, and it melted my heart.

In his first week here, Tathagata would seem nervous around us all, especially in the madness of the mealtimes. I took to seating him on my lap and feeding him.

'He's a boy, Bula. Don't mollycoddle him. You never had to do it with the girls.'

'Each child is different, Nikhil.'

'Treat them all the same and they will all turn out alike. This way you will just spoil him.'

'Nikhil, just let him be. Trust me.'

Tathagata took to calling us 'Nikhil' and 'Ma' just as the girls did. I tried to get him to call Nikhil 'Baba' but he would just stare at Nikhil a little warily, unable to make that leap. And for all his attempts at being a detached parent, Nikhil was now happier than he had ever been. It was as if a large hole in his being had now been filled. The indulgence may have been subdued but the pride and the joy were unmistakable. Never was it more visible than each night before retiring for bed, when he stood at the foot of his sleeping son's bed, with a sense of deep love and calm. I stood alongside him sensing that healing, that wholeness in Nikhil once again.

In time he grew into the pattern of our household. With the kids growing, the fun-loving spirit of Akhil and Niru, and Nikhil's love, the imposing mansion transformed into a warm vibrant home we all loved.

Akhil, Niru and the kids occupied the first floor. The nightclub designers had remodelled the entire floor into five custom designed bedrooms, an entertainment hall and a smart dining area. Nikhil and I were for very long now, the only occupants of the top floor. We had kept only five rooms in use. When home we spent all our waking time in Nikhil's study and the nights in my tiny bedroom saturated with memories. But each Saturday night Nikhil and I would sleep in the enormous, larger than king-sized bed in Nikhil's old bedroom.

Around eight each Sunday morning there would be fierce knocking on our door. I would be barely awake while Nikhil would go across to open the door. A strange procession would troop in. A bevy of maids first, bearing an elaborate breakfast for a dozen or so people. There would be three Labradors dancing about underfoot. The kids, all in their nightclothes, would come and sit on the bed. Akhil and Niru would saunter in carrying armloads of Sunday newspapers and find some more space on the bed among the kids, the food, the pillows and all.

'Time to wake up,' Nikhil would gently say and half-helping, half-supporting me would take me to the bathroom to brush my teeth. I would come back still groggy, protesting I wanted to sleep some more and was entitled to on my one day off, and huddle under my bedclothes. Nikhil would join me. He would prop up the pillows and sit up. He would scoop me onto his chest and hold me there. Food would be handled and dropped all over the bedclothes much to the delight of the dancing dogs to whom that offending piece of toast or sausage would be flung.

I would lie half asleep smiling on Nikhil's chest, his arm as strong as a promise around me. I would feel his heart beat steadily and his breath rise and fall evenly. I would feel a rush of love so powerful that I would come fully awake.

'Bula,' Nikhil would shake me gently. 'Make me a cup of tea. I can't handle this chaos without my cup of tea.'

And I would sit up; pouring tea for all the adults, making sure Nikhil got the first cup. Then I'd ruffle Tathagata's hair.

'How is my son this morning?'

He would smile up at me with quiet shining eyes. Sometimes he would say:

'I don't want to eat scrambled eggs, Ma.'

'Come baby, let me feed you.'

And I would.

'If that child ever needs to go to hostel, he is doomed to die of hunger,' Nikhil would say with a groan.

'All my kids will grow up smart and capable. Just you wait and see, Nikhil.'

Niru would read out in a monotone the weirdest news items he could find in the papers. Both he and Akhil were still highly indiscreet so Nikhil and I would clamp down on him like censors the moment we realised he was about to say something unsuitable for the kids. Akhil would tell me about some sweet I hadn't made him in a long time complaining that since I found Tathagata I had neglected him deplorably. I would give him a quick hug and reassure him that while Tathagata was one of three kids, he was my only brother and far more valuable. Geetanjali would sit close by Nikhil and the two of them would debate issues from the headlines of the papers. They share a magical bond and love each other profoundly. Debjani, the born manager, would be serving food efficiently to us all, scolding the dogs for jostling her.

✦ ✦ ✦

34

Bula: 46 years

We reached home around three.

'Let's go and see Ranga Ma.'

'She'll be resting now, I think.'

She wasn't. She was lying in bed watching live coverage of popular puja *pandals* on TV. Nikhil sat beside her on the bed.

'How are you? You should have come with us for lunch. The food was excellent. '

'Sometimes I should let you young people have fun on your own. Besides what can I eat outside? So many restrictions.'

'Akhil would have taken care. You know that, Ranga Ma. Do you want me to take you to the local pandal this evening?'

'We all went for the *anjali* this morning, didn't we? No need to go again. I'm enjoying watching all this on TV.'

Then she groped under her pillow and brought out something.

'Come, Bou-ma.'

I went closer and she fastened a heavily bejewelled bracelet to my wrist.

'This has been my favourite piece of jewellery. I haven't told you all how many I have lost already. This I can't bear to lose, so I had kept it hidden away. After all you have done for me, Nikhil, it is only fitting that I give it to Bula.'

Still sitting, Nikhil put an arm around my waist and holding my left hand, bent closer to look at the bracelet. A starburst of coloured gemstones winked up at us.

'It's beautiful, Ranga Ma.' And looking up at me with a smile, 'It suits you.'

When we left her room, we drifted into the informal drawing room. We hardly had time to use it anymore. But it was still warm with powerful reminiscences. Nikhil went and lay down on the day bed, moving towards the wall to make place for me beside him. I lay down with my cheek against his outstretched arm, facing him. His hand came up to feel my face.

'Tired?'

'No. You?'

'A little. I think I overate.'

I laughed.

'I think not having high-pressure work to attend to makes you a little disoriented.'

'And what would you suggest as a remedy?'

'Nothing, just lie like this and be nice to me.'

'Pity, I thought this room would bring out the romantic mood in you.'

His fingers traced the outlines of my face.

'Bula, do you realise we have been together for twenty five years now?'

'My farce of a marriage took place twenty five years ago. I think we got together more than four years after that. And then there was that infamous year you decided to abandon me.... It's only been twenty years of being together, Nikhil.'

Nikhil groaned.

'Why did I ever introduce you to accounting?'

For a moment both of us were silent drawn by our own thoughts. I lay with my head on his chest.

'Nikhil?'

'Hmmm?'

'Do you think our future will be as special as it has been all these years?'

'We have an excellent track record. We are two committed players. We have the expertise and the comfort levels. The environment around us is of more love and happiness than it has ever been. I really don't see why not.'

'Talking of the environment.... Did you notice Ma slipped into calling me Bula for the first time today?'

'I heard her call you that once before.'

'Really? When?'

'We were going somewhere. You were beside me and I was driving. Ranga Ma was in the back seat. We came upon this huge film hoarding with Reba undressed on it. None of us could avoid looking at it. And she said: 'Ignore it, Nikhil. As long as you have your Bula by your side, what do you care?'

'Yes, I remember now. We were holding hands then.'

'I think our being together would have been very difficult for her to accept for a number of reasons. She has been resigned to it for a very long time now though.'

'Yes. Yet today she seemed to have sanctioned it with this gesture of giving me her bracelet.'

'Did it matter to you?'

'In most ways, no. The only thing that really matters is you! Her acceptance is important as it validates what I believe in strongly that all external considerations fade when two people love each other deeply, powerfully.'

We lay chatting. The beauty of our relationship was that there was always something we wanted to tell the other, afresh, as each day unfolded and newer stronger emotions blossomed within us.

In a while I went to the door that opened out to the courtyard. I saw Sujoya outside the kitchen and called out to her. She came in bearing a laden tray.

The sounds of the drumbeats of the *dhak* from the nearby puja drifted up to us. There was a meaning and passion to the sound.

I held out a cup of tea to Nikhil.

He sat up with that smile that took my breath away and reached out to take it from me.

✦ ✦ ✦

Epilogue

Bula's Summation:

I am not a writer. I have only read extensively all my adult life. So I understand the value of books. They become close friends in the loneliest phases of our lives. And what we resist learning from our own lives, books may teach us. I decided to write this as a pledge: to try and propound that there really is no power stronger than that of love, in any form.

I am under no illusions. I know what I have written is crampingly sentimental, wrapped up in minutiae, so ordinary that it demands patience and tolerance from its reader. I have tried to replicate things as they unfolded the most faithfully I could. And so you would fault me too for sharing too many intimate details.

My story unfolds at a time in our cultural history when the ceremony of marriage was the finale of a woman's life. If the marriage proved dysfunctional, disastrous or led to an early widowhood, she was simply written off by all as a forgettable statistic. But in each such forgettable nameless figure, there lived a human being like me who really did not deserve what the fates and the others decided. The sense of honour demanded that she accept her reality and live in silence and deprivation. And truthfully that is what I had charted out for myself as well.

All around me there are women whose lives ended at the point at which mine really began. They were abandoned by those sworn to care for them. They continue living incredibly lonely lives only better than slaves in the households of men who married them for mistaken reasons and then discarded them. That is still scarily rampant as perverse power plays work out in the anonymity of households. It may seem liberalisation has brought greater freedom, greater respect to women.

Yet with greater freedom I see greater pain. I see people who really love, harming the most by simply being childish, unable to rise above themselves and their immediate concerns to forge lasting bonds of love. And that is why I think my saga with Nikhil is relevant.

Perhaps it is easy for me to say so because the fates gave me Nikhil. And as Debjani says, they don't make men like Nikhil any more.

As a damaged young woman, I had the access to a good soul like Nikhil by simply living in the same household. I encountered him on passages and at mealtimes, opening doors, running up the stairs, being out in the verandah and the gardens or simply slaving in the kitchen. There were family functions and festivals and just seeing him often was perhaps the happiest incidental of my otherwise miserable married life.

I regard it impossible for any unrelated young lady to have this kind of access to the wonder of Nikhil and yet not be drawn irresistibly. In the eyes of others I know it was a sin. The luxury to distinguish between sin and sanctity is denied to a few in situations like mine, utterly dispossessed, divested of all hope.

That does not mean that we had all the time and the freedom to romance each other. In our earlier interactions for months together, we did not speak or even encounter each other. We lived in a fairly confined space yet inhabiting disparate worlds which were monitored and kept apart by the people around us, not consciously, but out of convention. No one consciously did it simply because it was unimaginable then that a married woman would reach out to another man and even if she did, that any man would find anything remotely interesting in one plundered and disposed of.

One question recurs often. What prompted Nikhil to do the things he did? What did Nikhil ever see in me? He gives me many exquisite answers: a little unhappy that by persisting with this question, I seem to be plagued with doubts. And still this one thought perplexes me knowing as I do that though I had no options at all, he did and still chose me counter to all that seemed natural and sensible. I tell myself that in seeing me friendless and abused, desperately grappling to adjust to my cruel realities with dignity; he knew that I would perish without a saviour. He knew I needed him more than anyone ever would. And being a gentle evolved person he was, a universal giver, he took up that role.

The magic of Nikhil is that way back then, even when he had no clue who I was, he still saw me as a person, an interesting individual, someone to reach out to with love. To

Aukhoy Babu and his mother just my being poor was enough to condemn me. This dehumanising I am speaking of, was so extensive and nasty that when I write I cannot recall even one pleasant incident involving either of them.

Why would I want to write about sewing on a button or falling down in a faint with fever when Nikhil tended to me? Simply because these simple events were all I had; punctuating years of abuse and slaving in the kitchen for long rigorous hours.

In this narration I think I have not done justice to two very important entities – my daughters, and the beautiful mansion we lived in. When I first came into the mansion, its imposing beauty and grandeur frightened me. As with the painful experiences of my early days there, its vastness and shadowy corners made me nervous and homesick. In time it grew friendlier. I began to harmonise with its aspects. The mansion was sturdily built, high ceilinged and it has the most exquisite colonial furniture. Now it provides the most stunning backdrop to the unfolding beauty of love. On paper the mansion belongs to us: Nikhil and me. In reality, it is the mansion that has gracefully accepted my presence in it and given me its powerful shelter.

My daughters are central to my life. They are my pride and joy. However, they have not been central to this story and I regret that they appear even less than someone like Aukhoy Babu who I consider, without ill-feeling, as the most negligible entity in my life. As adults today my daughters have the right to ask many questions. They have never once asked me, why Nikhil? They have been supportive and understanding of our realities. They reciprocate the love Nikhil lavishes on them.

They do their best to keep our small circle of seven family members close-knit.

I marvel at how great all the kids are. Their earliest memories are not pleasant and that has made them appreciate everything nice that comes into their lives with greater warmth. The best part is that there was this unspoken agreement between Nikhil and me to bring them up as uncomplicated, middle class kids. They were given the simplest of joys – short weekend breaks at inexpensive hotels; sandwich and ice cream outings; shopping trips that only meant a visit to a bookstore or a gift shop if a birthday was coming up.

Debjani recounts this time when data on our company was used as a management case study on the power of traditional Indian family-run businesses vis-à-vis multinational corporates. Deetu skimmed through the figures and sat stunned only then realising how wealthy Nikhil, and by extension the family, was. Someone in the group began discussing the managerial acumen of Nikhil Mitra and she blurted out: 'Not really. I would know. Nikhil is my Dad.'

'Can't be. Your surname is Banerjee.'

'That's because we girls take our name from our Mom.'

And she took out her purse to show them all a family picture of all of us during a trip to the Sunderbans. The professor came up.

'Are you Nikhil Mitra and Bula Banerjee's daughter?'

She had nodded, only beginning to come aware of what that meant in the business world.

'You should ask them to come here and interact with all of us. We need this kind of industry exposure. Let's organise this talk sometime.'

Geetanjali grew up quiet and a little reserved. No one identifies with her as deeply as Nikhil for in some way their natures are mirrors of each other and they remain inseparably close today. Nikhil had insisted that all the kids take up tiny projects each vacation on some aspect of the company or its offices. And it helped all of them to have a very firm grasp on how things work and how to work in teams.

What happened to Aukhoy Babu, you may well ask? About a year after he was asked to leave, he returned penniless; turned away from every ashram he knew. His mother restored him to his room and tried unrelentingly to persuade Nikhil to let him stay. That very night Nikhil had him sent away to a hotel room. In the next fifteen days a spacious two-bedroom apartment was taken on long lease and Aukhoy Babu moved there with two houseboys and a handsome monthly allowance.

Still Aukhoy Babu came home for meals frequently when we were at office. He used to beg his mother for larger amounts of money each time, until he had completely eaten into her savings and she was compelled to refuse him any more. He took to just rifling through her drawers and taking bits of her jewellery, until one day she instructed the house help not to permit him entry into the household.

The twins visit frequently. And each time, they come laden with impossible amounts of goodies for all of us. They both chose to marry and settle in the States. And yet, they remain close, definitely calling us each weekend and keeping abreast of everything that is happening to all of us.

As soon as it was possible, way back, I took Nikhil on a getaway to my mother's house Phuleshwar. We spent happy hours there, especially unwinding in the garden among the many lush reed pools. As the kids grew we began taking them and later Akhil and Niru as well. They all loved the place. Often camping out on the extensive grounds.

On one of our visits, there was a signboard on Ashu's gate proclaiming that the place was for sale. All the men wanted to check it out, the thick mango groves looking even more beautiful with time. I dissuaded them saying I had reason not to want to do anything with that property. Nikhil let it go.

A couple of years later I was felicitated by the Women's Chamber of Commerce and a brief article on me appeared in a popular news magazine published out of Calcutta. I guess the name of the company was enough for people to know how to contact me.

Once, Nikhil was idly going through the pile of mail that sat on my desk.

'Bula, why would an Ashutosh Bhattacharya from Phoenix, Arizona be writing to you?'

'Ashutosh?'

'Hmmm.'

'He is someone I knew long ago, back in Phuleshwar.'

He dropped the letter back on my desk. When he came to collect me in the evening, he noticed the letter still sat unopened where he had left it.

'You've still not read the letter.'

'I don't want to.'

I tore it unopened and tossed the bits in the waste paper basket. As he started the car, Nikhil said:

'So, Ashutosh lived in the house with the mango orchards.'

I looked at Nikhil with a smile.

'Yes, he did. So long ago, that it simply doesn't matter anymore.'

One issue on which Nikhil and I have differences is Tathagata. He feels that I am unbalanced, over-protective and misguided in my love for him. And that unless he intervenes often to give the child a more realistic grounding, he will turn out spoilt.

There was something about Tathagata that made me want to just hold him and never let go. I possibly loved him the most among our three kids, unabashedly.

If forced to analyse this, I would come up with two insights.

In all my simple life I had tried my best not to harm or deprive anybody. Despite this principle I have always lived by, I did unwittingly displace Reba. In my overpowering love for Nikhil, I did commit this one offence. For a very long time, after each episode of exquisite lovemaking, I would say a small prayer begging God and Reba to forgive me my transgressions. In my blinding love for her son, I sought that forgiveness, that salvation.

The other factor was that I saw so much of Nikhil in Tathagata. Both were extremely handsome magnetic personalities but so different in looks that it was almost unbelievable that they were related. Yet I saw an air in Tathagata that I had seen in a very young Nikhil. It was a wistful air of being lonely and adrift. I strongly believe that Tathagata's choice of acting as a career had nothing to do with Reba and it was Nikhil's genes that made him gentle, sensitive and artistic. In holding and feeding and kissing Tathagata and giving him abundant love I was also reaching out to the Nikhil of the remote past who still lived in his son.

If I told Nikhil this, he would laugh it off.

'Madam, these are just excuses. For some unfathomable reason you love that kid more than anybody else in the world. It simply is. There are no deep explanations.'

'There is one flaw to your statement though, Nikhil.'

'Is there? What?'

'It's just that there does happen to be someone I love more than him.'

'There can't be.'

✦ ✦ ✦